EMBRACE MY HEART

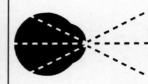

This Large Print Book carries the
Seal of Approval of N.A.V.H.

EMBRACE MY HEART

ALTONYA WASHINGTON

THORNDIKE PRESS
A part of Gale, Cengage Learning

GALE
CENGAGE Learning·

Farmington Hills, Mich • San Francisco • New York • Waterville, Maine
Meriden, Conn • Mason, Ohio • Chicago

GALE
CENGAGE Learning·

LIBRARY OF CONGRESS CATALOGING-IN-PUBLICATION DATA

Washington, AlTonya.
  Embrace my heart / by AlTonya Washington. — Large print edition.
    pages cm. — (Thorndike Press large print African-American)
  ISBN 978-1-4104-8158-0 (hardcover) — ISBN 1-4104-8158-1 (hardcover)
  1. African Americans—Fiction. 2. Large type books. I. Title.
PS3623.A86736E46 2015
813'.6—dc23   2015013833

Published in 2015 by arrangement with Harlequin Books S.A.

Printed in Mexico
1 2 3 4 5 6 7 19 18 17 16 15

To this mysterious, maddening
and marvelous thing called Love!

CHAPTER 1

Chasing a man wasn't something she did.

Come on, Vec, it's Qasim Wilder.

Vectra Bauer thinned her lips and tried to drive the silent reminder from her mind.

She guessed that most women would likely deem Qasim Wilder a man worthy of being chased.

Truth be told, Vectra herself could easily subscribe to the same notion if not for the fact that the man in question had been acting decidedly weird for the past few months.

They had enjoyed what she'd considered a pretty nice friendship until he had very noticeably begun to distance himself. As a woman who maintained a short list of close friends, Vectra couldn't afford to lose any — weird acting or not.

Which came to the point of her visit: chasing a man, indeed. She cast yet another speculative glance around the fortieth-floor private lobby outside the office for the president of Wilder. Qasim's financial savvy was as coveted as his looks. His name was so well known, his skills so respected, that there was no need to add additional wording to the business moniker.

Money was Qasim's game, and he was loved for it. *If only I were here to discuss business,* Vectra thought. She rubbed a clammy palm across the flaring hem of a casual cap-sleeved frock that hugged her unintentionally athletic figure.

She'd come to discuss a party, of all things. Vectra puffed out her cheeks and tried to preoccupy herself by attempting to count the cars crossing the Golden Gate Bridge, which stood in distinctive red splendor across the Bay. She managed to content herself with the fact that she at least didn't have to worry over being turned down. After all, she wasn't there to extend an invite.

The distinguished Mr. Wilder had made it very clear that a friendship with her was something he no longer had time for.

At least that was what his actions had suggested. Qasim had yet to come out and tell her what exactly had his boxers twisted. Rolling her eyes away from the stunning bridge, Vectra gave a mental sigh. Thoughts raging, she worked hard at putting her focus elsewhere. Periodicals were neatly arranged on a low marble coffee table set in the center of the lobby's upscale reception area. She wondered if she'd be waiting long enough to pick one of them and dive in.

"Vectra?"

It took a second or three for her to realize someone had actually called her name and that it hadn't been her trusty inner voice. She turned, an instant smile curving her mouth when she saw Qasim's assistant, Minka Gerald. She stood a few feet away from the large oak desk that occupied a spot in the workplace, which claimed almost the entire wall opposite an impressive line of floor-to-ceiling windows.

Minka quickly closed the distance between them. "Gosh, it's been forever!"

"It has." Vectra squeezed Minka's hands when the woman gave hers a shake. She could feel some of her apprehension dissolve as Minka's sunny demeanor worked its charms upon her.

"What are you doing waiting in the lobby?" Minka stopped squeezing Vectra's hands and tugged them insistently. "You'll be a lot more comfortable in Qasim's office."

"Minka . . ." Vectra bit her lip for an

9

instant. "I don't think that's such a good idea."

"Ah." Minka poked out her tongue and buzzed out a breath. "He's at lunch and won't be a bit happy to find you waiting in the lobby. Even if it *is* a private one."

Vectra didn't have the heart to tell the woman that what would probably make her boss happiest was for her not to be there at all. She decided against arguing. She was returning to the waiting area to collect her bag when a man arrived at Minka's desk.

"Mink! Sim around?"

"Hey, Will." Minka threw a smile over her shoulder. "He's still at lunch."

The man tapped the edge of the thin manila folder against his palm. He appeared to be weighing his options. "Any idea how long he'll be? I got some stuff for him to sign."

"Well, he left before I did." Minka secured her burgundy tote into a bottom drawer along the black credenza behind her desk. "I'm not sure how long he's been gone and when he *does* get back you'll still have to wait." She gave a slight nod past the man's shoulder.

"William Lloyd, Vectra Bauer," Minka made the introductions.

Will met Vectra between the waiting area

10

and Minka's desk, where he shook her hand. "Pretty sure Sim'll be much happier to see you here than me."

Vectra smiled, humored by the man's tease. "Don't count on it."

"Is there anything I can do, Will?" Minka offered.

"I don't see why not." Will turned, brows rising as his gaze crested above Minka's head. He grinned. "But no need to worry yourself."

"Sim." Minka laughed. "Great timing."

Vectra turned, too. She wasn't all that surprised to find Qasim Wilder wearing a dour expression, which he aimed directly at her. "Hey, Qasim," she managed, albeit softly.

"Vectra."

She could detect obvious surprise riddling Qasim's deep, soft voice. An edgier quality tempered the sound, however, before he seemed to lose all interest and completely dismissed her.

Qasim moved with his trademark stealth. An asset honed by his years in the military. He extended a hand toward the other man.

"Sorry for the bother, man." Grinning, Will heartily engaged in the handshake. "I need the go-ahead for a few things. Need your name on the line before I can move forward. Hotel people are some picky folk."

"What's up?" Qasim took the folder Will offered.

"Mostly pricing details. They want to know if I'm authorized to accept the quotes."

"All right." Qasim scanned the folder's contents. "I'll get this back to you soon." He passed the file to Minka. "Let's see about drafting a document for Will to have on hand as proof that I've given him the authority to make any decisions needed to organize this thing."

Minka smiled at Will. "I'll have the folder ready as soon as Sim has time to look it over. We'll have to give you a call once legal draws up the signing doc, okay?" She looked to her boss for approval.

Qasim's nod was confirmation enough and then he left the group.

Feeling thoroughly snubbed as he strolled off without another word, Vectra forbade herself from making one move. From the corner of her eye, she could almost see Minka and Will exchanging curious looks over Sim's slight. She gave a start when a loud knock echoed out over the space.

Qasim had returned to the lobby and was looking at Vectra from where he'd dropped the loud knock against the wall that shielded the long corridor leading to his office suite.

"You coming?" he called.

Vectra heard no hospitality in the words, only tense patience. She watched his inky-black stare scanning the length of her and wondered whether Minka or Will could read their boss's mind as easily as she did.

Apparently, they had noticed their boss's agitation. They quickly left her side. Minka returned to her desk.

"Nice to meet you." Will squeezed Vectra's arm on his way past.

"Same here," Vectra called to his departing figure.

She could have easily been amused by the sense of dread filling the area were she not the one caught in the crosshairs.

Qasim didn't wait for her to reach him at the corner of the hallway. Instead, he headed on down the carpeted, portrait-lined space. Vectra attempted to assess his mood as he walked before her. Not that his icy manner in the lobby hadn't been hint enough, but he acted like *she'd* been the one to go all antisocial when it'd been the other way around.

At any rate, it was no hardship to follow and observe him at a distance. Qasim's love for outdoor activity was evident even beneath his standard suit-and-tie work attire. That day, a walnut-brown three-piece suit adorned his toned, licorice-dark frame.

They had been friends long enough for her to know that he hated ties. He usually discarded whichever one he wore either just before or right after lunch. The guy loved his comfort and the fact didn't diminish the stunning craftsmanship of his body or face.

Bottomless dark eyes competed with the ebony richness of heavy brows and the sleep cap of hair he wore close cut. His facial hair was tamed into an intentional five o'clock shadow that partly hid a cleft chin and the faint lines that proved he was easy with his smiles.

Vectra blinked suddenly, at once regretting and realizing how much time she'd taken to admire the man's face and form. The fact made her wonder whether she'd subjected any of her other male friends to such scrutiny. Doubtful. Her male friends were just that — just friends. Or, rather, they had been . . . until she met Qasim; he was a male friend she would have preferred become much more.

He opened one of the towering maple doors leading to his office. Vectra quickened her pace when she realized he was going to hold it for her as though she were an actual welcomed visitor. In spite of his polite manners, however, she could've sworn she picked up on a low yet distinctive sound of agitation. That sound rumbled through his chest when she passed him on her way into the room.

If ever there was an office that personified its owner, it's Qasim's, she thought.

The place was a testament to pretty much everything he held dear. One far, expansive corner was a hive of activity with wide-screen monitors broadcasting both financial and sports news from their perches atop a pair of pristine maple desks. Towering bookcases lined the room and were filled with pictures, plaques, awards and books spanning a range of genres. Above the cases nearest the desks was a stock ticker.

Vectra set her tote on one of the square black leather chairs that surrounded an impressive gaming area. She wondered if nice or nasty was the way to begin their conversation. She didn't have long to debate.

"Coming to invite me to another party, Vec?"

The words carried over Qasim's broad shoulder as he headed into his work area. He removed his suit coat, slung it over the back of the sofa he passed and smiled in her direction when he turned.

Okay, then . . . she decided, accepting that the conversation would be a tad strained. "Actually, I came to ask why I've been selected as the lucky one to get the brunt of the petty side of your personality?"

He smiled. While the gesture held a great deal of humor, the air of agitation remained.

"Qasim?" Vectra's attempt to remain steely gave way, and her curiosity got the better of her. "Why are you angry with me?" She didn't care for the pleading tone that clung to her words, but she wanted answers.

Qasim appeared taken aback, but recovered soon enough. "I'm not angry with you." He made a pretense of reviewing the folders lying open on his desk.

"Well, you're something. What'd I do?" Curiosity had given way to a smidge of self-consciousness while she stood before him. Something changed. His smile was gone, and the look that replaced it was observant in a way that made Vectra flush with heat.

Another of the agitated rumbles surged in Qasim's chest, and he pushed back the wide black leather chair behind his desk.

Vectra could hear nothing over her heart beating wildly as anticipation had its way with her.

Qasim didn't take a seat in the chair; instead, he headed in Vectra's direction and

16

then shifted toward the maple wet bar, which displayed a wide array of liquor bottles in various shapes and sizes.

Quietly, Qasim went about preparing Vectra's vodka tonic, which he set firmly upon the bar top. From the full-size black fridge behind him, he retrieved his beer of choice and popped the top.

He tipped the bottle to his mouth. "I'm not angry with you."

Vectra stood in place, nervously rubbing her fingers together while she observed Qasim with a wary gaze. He motioned with his bottle for her to take the vodka. Vectra didn't care how eagerly she accepted. The drink went a long way in calming her ridiculously frazzled nerves.

The lush line of Qasim's mouth grew even lusher as a smile emerged. She rolled her eyes. "You said that already, so excuse me for not believing you." She gave him her back, keeping the drink clutched securely between her hands.

Qasim allowed his emotions greater purchase while Vectra's back faced him. He didn't realize the blackness of his stare softened as it always did when just the mere thought of her stirred.

He watched her sip from the glass but noticed that she didn't empty it. She put more distance between them, which gave him time to absorb the missed sight of her.

The more time they spent together, the more she stunted his ability to properly think or even speak. He'd masked it for as long as he could. When he could no longer do that, he latched on to his only option.

Because he didn't want to be her friend. He wanted much more.

She finished her drink and turned on him. "You shut me out. I thought we were friends and then you — you stopped calling, stopped *taking* my calls. Why? What'd I do?"

Qasim took another swig of his beer and gave a half shrug. "Guess you won't accept the 'it's not you, it's me' defense?"

"No." She produced a cool smile and set her glass on the bar with more force than needed. "And I've got a good conversation starter since clearly you can't get the discussion going. Robb's party? It's tonight. When we spoke a while ago, I got the impression that you didn't have a date, either, so I thought we could go together. When you shot me down, I decided to ask someone else. He turned me down, too, but thankfully he told me *why* he had to say no before I ran off to embarrass myself by asking someone else."

"Lew?" At her confirming nod, Qasim

rolled his eyes.

Lewis Olin was a mutual friend who struggled with the concept of keeping secrets. While people tended to admire the man's honesty, they often found the trait to be a nuisance.

"Why don't you want anyone else to take me to the party?" Her voice was quiet.

"I didn't tell him that." Qasim finished his beer and turned to the bar fridge for another just to have a reason to shield the truth from his eyes.

"No, Qasim, you told Lew you'd break his hand before he could press the send button when he mentioned calling me to ask me to Robb's party. Why would you say that?"

"I didn't mean it." Silently, though, Qasim feared that the threat had been all too real at the time. He lost his taste for the second beer, slamming the fridge door shut to round on her. "You're an idiot if you don't know why I wouldn't want anyone else to take you out."

"I'm no idiot, Sim." *At least not about that.* "I just want to hear you say it."

"I can't be your friend." Qasim pushed off the bar, massaging the bridge of his nose.

Vectra blinked twice in rapid succession. The words were like a slap, yet they hadn't rendered her speechless. "You can't be my friend and you don't want anyone else to be my friend, either?"

Qasim was returning to his desk when her accusation reached his ears. Her voice carried a lost chord, forcing him to turn and face her. He couldn't speak for simply wanting to look and to fantasize.

The woman had too many male friends who were *just* friends. While that fact pleased him, it had unfortunately given her the false perception that any man she categorized as such would remain true to the label and want nothing more.

He'd known he was unworthy of the friendship title from the day he met her.

Hell, who could blame me? he thought, fully allowing himself to appreciate her.

He knew she had an unnatural disdain for exercise. The lack of activity seemed to have had no adverse effects on her body, though. Her svelte figure was encased beneath a dress that emphasized shapely legs that he'd dreamed of having wrapped around his back. Her breasts were ones he very much wanted bared to his gaze.

Her dark hair was cropped into a pixie cut. The chic style accentuated the oval beauty of her rich, caramel-toned face. Further illuminating her features was a hauntingly lovely pair of walnut-brown eyes.

"Qasim?" Vectra snapped her fingers in front of his eyes.

She had moved closer, stopping inches before where he'd taken a seat on the edge of his desk. His reflexes were swift, and he captured her wrist, which caused her to bite her lip in an attempt to hide a gasp.

"You have a habit of underestimating your so-called friends," he said.

"Obviously." She tried to tug her wrist free of his hold. "Not everyone is like you, Qasim. Some people know what it's like to be a friend." She decided to lash out with her words as breaking free of Qasim's grip was rather out of the question.

He stood, smiling down ill-humoredly from his height advantage. "Some people know what it's like to be a friend, Vec, but I don't think you have a clue what it's like for a man to be friends with a woman when he can't be."

He released her so suddenly that Vectra stumbled a little. She let the momentum propel her toward the chair where her tote bag lay. Grabbing a handle, she made it to the office door and left it swinging open in the wake of her departure.

CHAPTER 2

Qasim returned to his desk once Vectra had stormed out. He braced one hand on the edge to support his weight, but he refused to sit.

He'd hurt her — deeply. While it hadn't been his proudest moment, he hoped she'd stay away from him as a result. He wasn't a complete dunce; he knew she was attracted to him and sensed it had occurred to her that he knew.

A few months ago, he'd decided to pull back. She was pissed at him now, but the circumstances of their current situation were far more favorable than the one she'd have to deal with when she discovered how in over her head she could be with him. The very last thing he wanted was for her to fear him. She surely would if she realized how deep his attraction to her really went.

There was a quick knock and a second's hesitation before the office door opened a sliver. Minka stuck her head in. "Is it safe in here?" she called, her small round face carrying an uncertain smile. "What'd you do? Vectra looked ready to kill somebody when she walked out of here."

"I told her the truth." Qasim claimed the big chair behind his desk. "She's got no idea what it'd mean to be 'friends' with a man like me."

"And I'm guessing you let it end there and didn't bother to tell her what you really meant?"

"I don't want her afraid of me, Mink."

"And because of that, you're not willing to give her the benefit of the doubt?" Minka spread her hands apart in a what-the-heck gesture. "So you don't like the idea of other men around her. A lot of women would find that an attractive trait."

"Would you?" he challenged.

Minka shrugged. "I . . . I think I'd enjoy it. Yeah." She sighed, smiling smugly. "I'd feel secure, treasured, as long as the guy didn't get too weird about it." She stopped when Qasim ticked a finger in her direction as though she'd said something magical.

"That's it. I don't know how weird I'd get considering the fact that yesterday I threatened a very good friend for just wanting to pick up the phone and call her."

"Ouch . . . Not good." Minka scrunched her nose.

"This is worse. He told her all about it." Qasim closed his eyes, rested his head against the chair's high back. "He's one of those 'honesty is the best policy' folks."

"Sometimes it is." Minka smiled. "With things being more out in the open, she won't let you hide behind the 'we can't be friends and that's that' argument."

Qasim worked the bridge of his nose between thumb and forefinger. "You don't understand."

"You're right. I don't. I mean, what's the problem?" Minka claimed a spot on one of the sofa arms. "Vectra's gorgeous, funny, smart. The men who work for you make a point of stopping by the office when they know she's in the building."

The news didn't set well with Qasim if the muscle flexing wildly along his jaw was any indication. He lowered his hand, letting his elbow rest along one of the chair's wide arms. He looked toward Minka with keen interest and much humor. "Is that why Will really stopped by?"

"No." Minka laughed. "He really does need those signatures." She reached for the folder she'd brought in with her. "It's probably a good thing that he decided to drop by." She went to hand her boss the paperwork. "It's become a lot more expensive to host charity events these days."

"Hmph." Qasim opened the folder. "When there's a charity that brings in millions, everyone wants their cut."

"So you agree it's a waste of money?"

"A waste of money for a good cause," Qasim countered, sleek brows united to form a studious frown.

"So who says we have to waste it? Why don't you just have the thing at your place?"

"Not big enough."

"Says the man living in the two-million-dollar condo." Minka shook her head. "How about your place at Sea Cliff?"

"Don't like it."

Minka gasped. "Says the man living in the *four*-million-dollar house!"

"All right, then." Qasim smiled indulgently. "I admit I just don't want the aggravation of it. There's a certain convenience in not using your own place as the venue. Besides, neither of those places is right for accommodating that many people for a long weekend, hence the reason I always use hotels for this."

Qasim's midyear charity event was a highly anticipated gathering that benefited the summer camps he held each year for

25

deserving high school football players. Thanks to the funds raised by Qasim's Wilder Warriors Foundation, deserving students and senior athletes were able to receive all-expenses-paid educations following graduation.

Qasim watched his assistant, who didn't seem to be in full agreement with his reasoning. "Hell, Mink, are the rates that bad?"

"I believe so. Yes." She waved toward the folder he studied. "The venues we have in mind are even more outrageous than usual."

Although Qasim wasn't above paying any cost to fund his events, Minka saw to it that her boss's generous heart didn't bankrupt him. Her policy was to see to it that all charity expenses were paid from charity money allotted for such spending instead of directly from Qasim's personal accounts. She had successfully made that happen since the onset of Qasim's goodwill endeavors.

"The rates aren't deal breakers, but . . ."

"So go for it," Qasim urged.

"It's just —"

"Are the expense accounts well-funded?"

"More than. Only . . ." Minka trailed off, watching Qasim reach for a pen to sign the documents up for debate.

He smiled, noticing that his efficient assistant had already included a drafted document for the legal department to review regarding Will Lloyd's decision-making authority for the foundation.

"Very nice," he commented upon scanning the page.

Minka slipped off the sofa arm and took a bow. "Thanks and for my next feat, I'll get things straightened out between you and Vectra."

The easy expression Qasim was working to maintain began to waver. He clenched a fist and groaned. "I don't think there's any trick that good."

"Sim —"

"I appreciate the effort, but there's a lot you don't know. It's not my place to discuss it."

"So you deny going after the woman you love and deny any other man the chance to go after her."

Qasim shuffled through papers on his desk without really seeing them. "I don't want to think about it."

Minka walked over and took the folder from his desk. "She may not give you a choice." Waving the folder, she turned on her heel. "I'll get this finished."

Qasim fixed his gaze on the fist he'd

clenched before he slammed it onto his desk.

Vectra had never been one to take hints exceptionally well. She usually had to be hit right in the face with something before she got wise to the situation. She couldn't help but think that was the case now. His words and demeanor were giving off the distinct impression that there was someone else.

Boy, wasn't that the literal truth, she thought while speeding down the winding dirt road leading to Carro.

Named for Vectra's parents Oscar and Rose Bauer, Carro was a remarkably breathtaking wine-country estate in Saint Helena, California. It was Vectra's home and her oasis — a place for rejuvenation and meditation. A place to hide? She shook off that difficult truth and then thought, *What the hell?* So what if she wanted to hide? It was time to retreat a little.

She'd had her fill of humiliation. Qasim Wilder was a man who didn't want to be friends with her. Fair enough. Fair enough. Only . . . Well, jeez, he had to know she wanted more than that. She should've told him so long ago. Now, she was happy that she hadn't. Humiliating, indeed, once he had given her such a polite brush-off. Of course, there may *not* have been someone else had she not been too much of a coward to tell him that she'd wanted their friendship to take a more beneficial turn.

Vectra parked her luxury crossover a short distance from the turnoff leading to the main house. Leaving the vehicle, she walked a few feet to the wooden fencing that marked the entrance to Carro's lush vineyards.

Unmindful of her pumps, Vectra propped a foot on one of the planks that constructed the massive fencing. Resting her elbows on the top plank, she bowed her head and made a weak attempt at working the kinks from her neck. She inhaled, at once comforted by the fragrant air kissed by the plump, sweet fruit that clustered about vibrant green vines.

The Carro land had been in Vectra's mother's family for centuries. Rose was a descendent of the Pomo Tribe, one of several Native American tribes that called Sonoma home. Rose had come from a family that understood the value of their land and defended their right to keep it.

That very land had been the dowry Rose Wolf had brought with her when she met and married Oscar Bauer, a young African-American agriculture consultant who had been making a name for himself among area farmers. He'd brought his skills from the North Carolina farm country he'd called home. In time, he built a respected business that thrived and diversified once he and his wife joined forces to cultivate the property.

The Bauers had managed to cultivate more than a respected vineyard for themselves and their surrounding neighbors. They'd cultivated what many would call an enchanted life for their two children. Vectra never had a shortage of friends, primarily the children of the adults who worked her family's land.

It had been Vectra's athletic, outdoorsy personality that had brought her more male than female playmates.

"Right . . ." Vectra inhaled deeply, willing the air to work more of its magic on her mood. "Outdoorsy, yes. Athletic . . . Not so much now," she criticized herself, but felt comforted by the fact that she still had her friends. At least, *she* considered them friends. Qasim obviously disagreed.

The visit to his office had gone nothing like she'd planned. For weeks, she'd wanted to confront him about withdrawing from their relationship, but had resisted the urge. Discovering the way he'd threatened one of their friends had given her courage to confront him. She'd hoped to get him to tell her why he'd done it and in turn spark a discussion about what more could exist between them.

Sadly, the conversation had derailed and she had no idea how to get it back on track. At least she'd gotten out of there without making an even greater fool of herself. He'd met someone. Someone he *was* interested in being more than friends with.

A horn honked and she looked back, a sunny grin appearing when she spotted the Jeep behind her car and the man inside. She waited, watching her brother hop out from the driver's side.

Oliver Bauer glanced at her car. "Are you on your way in or out?" He opened his arms wide to greet his baby sister and gave her a hug.

"Just getting back from the city."

Vectra relished the embrace but reminded herself not to lean in to the reassuring hold for too long. She didn't need Oliver questioning her mood. Her brother and father already worried too much over her.

"All the way from Frisco? Gallery business?" he asked, referring to one of two galleries Vectra owned.

"Just went to see a friend." She shrugged. "Needed to shop for Robb DeWitt. His

31

birthday party's tomorrow night, you know?"

"Yeah, yeah, I got an invite." Oliver nodded, rubbing his jaw as he spoke.

"Who are you taking?" Vectra kicked at a loose thatch of grass and dirt, attempting faint interest.

"Not sure I'm even going." Oliver rolled the sleeves of a black denim shirt over heavily corded forearms. "Guess you are?"

"I am."

"Good for you." Oliver gave her a sidelong glance. "You good?"

"Yeah . . . yeah, yeah." She shifted her weight and cringed. "I just waited too long to get a date. I may have to go solo."

"Solo." Oliver made a face and moved past his sister to recline against the plank fence. "So *all* the good guys were taken, huh?"

"Not *every* good guy." Vectra joined her brother, bracing her elbows against the fence and gazing up at him with an adoring smile.

Oliver grunted a laugh, his light, deep-set eyes reflecting more vibrancy in the sunlight. "The flattery, while true, will get you nowhere."

Vectra rolled her eyes. "Tell me about it."

"What about Qasim?"

32

She did a double take, put distance between her and Oliver. "Where'd *that* come from?"

Oliver merely shrugged off the question.

Vectra reciprocated the gesture. "I already asked him, anyway. He turned me down."

"Seriously? He really turned you down?" Oliver looked incredulous.

Vectra's smile reflected sympathy. "He really did, but it's fine. I understand why he had to. He's seeing someone."

Oliver's incredulous expression seemed to intensify into devastation. "He told you that?"

"He didn't have to, Olive." Vectra slapped her hands to her thighs and turned to take in the view beyond the fence once more. "He doesn't want to be friends anymore — told me so himself — said he *couldn't* be. Isn't that male-speak for 'I'm seeing someone else'?"

"I don't know, Vecs . . . I think you might be way off."

"Well . . ." Vectra dismissed the issue with an airy wave.

"So? Are you still gonna go even though no one asked you?"

Vectra accepted her brother's good-natured ribbing with a laugh. "I already told Robb I'd go, and I'm having a new gallery

33

event soon." She shrugged, inhaled the fragrant air and sighed. "It'll be good to get out and be seen before that."

"New gallery thing, huh?" Oliver nodded approvingly. "That'll be good for you. We — me and Dad — were wondering what your plans were for the place. You haven't been spending a lot of time at either location."

"Guess I have been a little preoccupied," Vectra admitted. She kept quiet about the fact that it was because she'd been more interested in being available for Qasim Wilder whenever he called.

Oliver nudged her elbow.

"I suppose I could lower my standards yet again and take you since I haven't had the time to get a better date."

"Well, I appreciate your sacrifice!" Vectra laughed. "I'll be sure not to depend on you for a ride home, though."

"You offend me, Vecs." Oliver planted a hand to the middle of his chest. "So it sounds like we have a date, but let me know if you get a better offer."

"Doubtful." Flashbacks of her chat with Qasim came to mind. She pulled back from the fence. "I'm heading to the house. You coming?"

Oliver gave a theatrical sigh while strolling with his sister. "Since I got nothin' better to

34

do." He groaned upon receiving a shove for his honesty.

"I'll meet you at the house." Vectra tugged Oliver with her as she headed to her car, but her steps slowed the nearer she drew to it. "Olive? Why are you out here? Just in the area?" Her brother lived in San Francisco.

Oliver shrugged beneath the shirt he sported. "You've got your ex-friend to thank for that. Sim called me."

She stilled. "Why?"

"He told me you guys had a not-so-nice conversation. Didn't tell me what it was about, but he said you were upset and he wanted me to check on you. I was up at the marketing park," he said, referring to the administrative offices for Carro Vineyards, "so it didn't take long to drive over."

It all still triggered Vectra's curiosity. "That's a little extreme, don't you think?"

"He's protective of you. I get that."

Vectra smiled, albeit sadly, understanding her brother's meaning. "You and Dad have reason to be protective — even if it does drive me out of my mind."

"Qasim isn't like that bastard who put his hands on you, Vec. I don't profess to be able to read the man's mind, but I don't think he'd ever put his hands on a woman that way."

Vectra entwined her fingers with Oliver's. "Neither do I," she said, feeling a slight chill as memories of an unfortunate and long-dead relationship came to mind.

"He doesn't even want to be my friend. Why bother?"

"Maybe the friendship role isn't the one he was aiming for." Oliver winked, leaned in to drop a kiss to his sister's cheek. "See you at the house."

Vectra watched her brother sprint over to hop into the Jeep and drive away in a flurry of dust. She leaned against the hood of her ride and delved into a bit of deep thought.

He doesn't want to be my friend, doesn't want any of my other friends to call or even take me out. He has my brother drive over to check on me afterwards . . . What the hell kind of game is he playing?

She was more than familiar with the protective — well, overprotective — element, being a direct recipient of it from her father and brother. Not wanting her to go out with anyone else, though? That held traces of possessiveness that she knew could be signs of other things . . .

She shook her head, reaching around to massage the knotted muscles at her nape. Qasim wasn't like that. She knew him well enough, had enough . . . past experience to know that wasn't in his nature.

There was something up with him, though, and she was too curious about what it was to let fear of humiliation stop her from getting to the bottom of it.

CHAPTER 3

"Great." Vectra veiled the murmured phrase behind a tight smile. She found herself in San Francisco again the next morning, having arranged to meet her father for breakfast. She hadn't expected to find him with his investment banker.

Qasim caught sight of her before Oscar Bauer realized his daughter had arrived. Whatever Qasim had been saying was silenced midsentence and he purposefully scanned Vectra's body, which was encased in a curve-hugging magenta frock.

Vectra had but a moment to flash her father a greeting smile before he was completely eclipsed by Qasim when he approached her.

"Are you okay?" He'd invaded Vectra's space, sending her back until her shoulder brushed the wall she stood closest to in the bar entryway of the bistro.

Her tight smile returned. "I'm all right,"

she lied.

"Baby!" Oscar Bauer pulled his daughter into a crushing hug and then set her back to give her an adoring once-over. Satisfied, he reached up to clap Qasim's shoulder. "Have this guy bring you to our table when you're done." He shook hands with Qasim then. "We'll get together for drinks next week."

"Sounds good, sir." Qasim dropped his free hand over the one shaking Oscar's.

"Thanks for sending Oliver out to check on me," Vectra said once her father had walked on. She observed him closely, waiting to glimpse his response and hoping she'd taken him enough by surprise to get an honest reaction.

Qasim only offered the barest hint of a smile. "You're welcome." He offered her his arm. "Your dad's waiting."

She refused his arm. "That's it?"

The smile ghosting around his alluring mouth gained definition.

Vectra blinked owlishly. "Is that a thing men do for women they don't want to be friends with?"

She never knew whether he'd planned to respond. They were interrupted when a slender, attractive, dark-blond man jostled Qasim.

"Sorry, guy, thought I'd be late," the man explained, his expression softening a bit further when he saw Vectra. "Well, well, what's up, pretty lady?"

Vectra left off the budding tension-filled conversation to greet Austin Sharpe with a hug and cheek kiss.

"What's goin' on? How's the fam?" Austin kept an arm about Vectra's waist while making his inquiries.

While they chatted and carried on like the old friends they were, Qasim worked to keep his temper at bay. Jaw clenched, he hid a fist in a deep trouser pocket.

". . . and I wanted to talk to you about putting together a cocktail party at your gallery," Austin was saying.

Vectra's cocoa eyes sparkled. "I like it. It'd be a perfect segue for an upcoming show I'm planning. You might want to send someone over to check the place out, make sure it's right for what you've got in mind."

"Actually, Vec, it's the Miami gallery I'm interested in."

Her eyes were positively luminous. "Now you've got my attention. Why don't we get together and discuss it?"

Austin patted the small of her back. "I'll call to see what your schedule's like. Are your numbers still the same?"

"They are. How long will you be around?"

"I'm trying to work about three deals." Austin smoothed a hand across his close-shaven jaw and grinned sheepishly. "That's why I'm meeting with *this* guy." He jerked a thumb in Qasim's direction. "Killing all my birds with the same stone and I'm even heading out to Robb's party tonight."

"Me, too." Vectra slapped Austin's arm.

He eyed her speculatively. "Guess I don't need to ask whether you've got a date already?"

Vectra used a flippant shrug as her response. "Hope that doesn't mean you won't come? I'll be there, and I'm sure my date won't mind us talking for a while."

"Mr. Wilder?"

Qasim, Austin and Vectra turned toward the host who had interrupted.

"Your table's ready, sir," the man announced.

Austin squeezed Vectra's arm once the host had moved on. "I'll take what I can get. See ya tonight." He kissed her cheek, clapped Qasim's arm. "See you at the table, man."

"Shall we?" Vectra looked from Qasim to the dining room and back again.

"You've got a date to Robb's party?" he asked.

Smug, Vectra leaned close, pretending to straighten Qasim's tie. "Guess you didn't get around to scaring everybody away from me."

Qasim brought his hands to her waist, cupping her hips firmly enough to keep her still before him. "Don't play this game with me, Vectra."

"It's not a game I started, Qasim, and since games aren't my style, consider this as me coming clean." She moved closer, silently commanding herself not to swoon over the feel of his hands on her body.

"We were friends. Good ones. I wanted more — by *more*, I mean that I wanted to sleep with you. You had to know that." She searched his bottomless eyes for a moment before she continued. "Yeah . . . I believe you did, and you withdrew anyway. I can accept that, but then you tell everyone else to stay away from me like I've got the plague? No, Qasim, I'm not playing a game. I only have questions. I'm guessing the answers aren't all that easy for you to give."

She glanced toward his hands, smothering her waistline. "Excuse me?" She waited, walking away when he released her.

The attentive server smiled engagingly while Austin Sharpe praised Qasim for his banking skills. She then laughed good-naturedly when Qasim told her that given all the money he was making Austin she should expect him to leave her an outrageous tip.

"Seriously now, man, about these investments. Should I buy stock in all three?" Austin queried while adding a wealth of cream to his coffee.

"Not all three."

"Uh-oh." Austin grinned. "So which one didn't make the cut?"

Qasim stirred his preferred black coffee. "None of them made the cut."

Austin stilled, the mug halting halfway to his mouth. "You're kidding?"

"No . . . but I could if you just really have a need to throw good money away on worthless stock."

"Forget I asked." Austin sipped on the beige-hued coffee.

"So what's goin' on in Miami?"

"New investors I'm trying to woo." Austin pushed at the shock of blond hair that consistently fell across his forehead. "I want a mixer that's off the beaten path, hence me wanting to use Vectra's gallery in Miami Beach."

"I didn't know you knew her that well." Qasim managed the comment in spite of his clenching jaw.

Austin nodded amidst a chuckle. "I was an intern for her dad's company — the man's brilliant. I have a lot of respect for Oscar Bauer."

"Second that," Qasim added.

"Hmph . . . for all the good it did me." Austin sounded playfully distressed.

Qasim tilted his head. "How so?"

Austin shrugged. "Well, it's important to bond with the father of your intended," he smiled, "but that was useless since I fell into the dreaded realm of friendship." He looked up as if to measure Qasim's reaction. "You know what I mean."

Qasim toasted the man with his mug. "Explain it to me."

"Look at her, Sim." Austin nodded across the sun-strewn dining room where Vectra sat with her father. "I mean, what guy in his right mind would want to be 'just friends' with her?"

Qasim felt his eyelids grow heavy beneath the weight of unexpected agitation and knew a bit more effort was warranted to maintain his cool. "Are you telling me that if you had the chance, you'd show her why she was making a mistake putting you in that category?"

Austin's expression changed to one that was unwaveringly serious. "As much as I'd enjoy a physical relationship with her, I'd never want her afraid to have me as a friend." He shook his head, sending the blond shocks of hair tumbling across his brow again. "She trusts me. I'd never do anything to jeopardize that."

Qasim barely nodded. "That's good to hear." Beneath the table, he unclenched the fist he hadn't realized he'd made.

"Just put one of those little packets on the side."

"Daddy. No."

"What's it gonna hurt?"

Vectra looked at their waitress. "Thanks, Kelly, that'll do it. No salt packets for my dad."

"Yes, ma'am." Kelly Dawes hid a smile as she scribbled something on her pad. "Sorry, Mr. B.," she quietly tacked on before hurrying off to place the breakfast orders.

"Party pooper," Oscar Bauer grumbled. "Now I remember why I rarely ask you out to eat anymore."

"Hmph." Vectra pretended to pout. "And I thought it was because you preferred my home cooking."

Oscar snorted. "That, too." He grinned and pulled his daughter close for another hug and kiss.

45

"So tell me about this trip of yours." Vectra propped her chin on the backs of her hands. "Did you even take a little time out to just play around?"

Some of the light doused in the man's long, expressive gaze. "You know playing around doesn't have the same punch it used to when I had your mother to do it with."

As far as Oscar Bauer was concerned, there was no woman he craved by his side other than his wife, but Rose had passed eight years prior.

"So did you give in to your obsession to acquire more land, or were you able to resist?" Vectra asked, eager to pull their thoughts away from sorrow.

"I only window-shopped." An amused light began to creep into Oscar's eyes, but not completely. "I wanted your advice before making any final decisions."

"Dad?" Surprised, Vectra laughed a little.

"I'm serious, baby. It's a place I could see spending the rest of my days. If it staggers you the way it did me when I saw it —" he shrugged "— then I'll know I've found my spot. You've got your mother's draw to the land. I'll trust your reaction to it."

"You've intrigued me, Daddy." Vectra sighed in a mock haughty tone before she sobered. "Do you think the visit could wait

46

until after this gallery show I've got coming up? I've got to visit the Miami gallery, anyway. I could detour and check out your spot before I do that."

"Fantastic." Oscar gave a single clap. He fixed her with an approving look and smile. "I see you haven't been resting on your laurels while I was away."

"Don't you mean I haven't been 'hiding out'?"

"I didn't say that." Oscar shifted to a newer, more comfortable position in his chair. "But since *you* did, then yes. Yes, I am *very* glad to know that. I was concerned after talking to Oliver last night."

"Right." Vectra served up a rueful smile, at last realizing the true motivation behind the sudden invite to breakfast. "What, Dad? Did he tell you he was taking me to Robb's party tonight?"

Oscar retrieved a minitablet from his inside suit coat pocket. "He may have mentioned it."

"Daddy!"

"All right, all right, we talked about it, and just so you don't go off trying to kill the boy, he actually stood up for you — told me he didn't think there was anything we needed to be concerned about. You know how we get about you, baby. What you went through before . . . it did a number on us, too, you know?"

Vectra squeezed her father's hand. The server returned with coffee for Oscar and tea for Vectra. She helped herself to several sips, waiting for the herbal blend to work its magic on the nerves her father and brother could so easily rattle with their overprotective natures.

Vectra didn't hold it against them. They had every right to be protective of her after the nightmare she'd lived through. The fact that she hadn't told them about it simply increased their tendency to worry that she'd suffer alone. She had discovered, though, that San Francisco and its surrounding areas encompassed a surprisingly small world. The Bauers were well-known. Word of her ex-boyfriend's abuse, when he had taken to shaking her viciously during an argument in a popular restaurant, had quickly reached Oscar and Oliver.

"Daddy, I'm good. I'm doing fine, really." She leaned in closer to him. "I only asked Olive to take me because I waited around too long before deciding I even wanted a date to the thing, and then all the good ones were taken."

"I find that hard to believe." Oscar scanned the dining room before looking her way again. "You and Sim seemed pretty close earlier."

"Daddy . . ."

"Apologies, apologies." Oscar raised his hands in a show of phony defense. "You know I have a soft spot for the boy. That's one I wouldn't mind for a son-in-law."

"Hmm . . . and could that be because he has a talent for making you money?"

"No." Oscar sounded playfully indignant and then he grinned. "Not entirely."

He sobered, squeezing Vectra's wrist.

"I know what a man looks like when he's hopelessly around the bend for a woman. That's the way Qasim Wilder looks when he looks at you." Oscar shared his sage observation and then turned his focus toward the tablet, grinning when he found what he wanted.

"Lake Misurina, Italy," he announced. "My *hopeful* retirement destination. Did you know that the last time Olympic speed skating was held on natural ice, *this* was the place it was held?"

"No, I —" Vectra blinked, working to fix her attention on the screen. "I didn't know that." She concentrated on what she was looking at, difficult given her thoughts were almost wholly centered elsewhere.

■ ■ ■ ■

Qasim resisted the urge to order a straight shot of whiskey to chase his bacon and eggs. He watched Austin Sharpe head over to speak to his former mentor Oscar Bauer. Qasim habitually gritted his teeth when the man made a point of drawing Vectra into his arms while he chatted with her father. He'd already clenched his fists until his arms had grown numb. Unfortunately, looking away from the cozy scene across the room didn't seem to be an option for him.

A dull ache hit his jaw when he recommitted to grinding his teeth. The sight of Austin patting Vectra's hip promised to drain whatever restraint Qasim had lorded over his temper.

To say he had it bad for her seemed a pathetic description of how wildly his emotions raged when she was in his presence. He had a possessive nature that had always been a part of who he was. As a kid who really didn't have much to be possessive of growing up, he had taught himself to stifle those emotions. It had been relatively easy. Growing up underprivileged, he had learned to wear the face of a kid who was anything but. That was before the hard work, which

50

had brought success and wealth, allowed a modicum of those emotions to resurface, and he had indulged himself.

Even still, that possessiveness had been in relation to *things.* Never had it crept over to another person — a woman. Only to himself could he admit the slight fear his possessiveness had the tendency to instill. He and Vectra had struck up a friendship that had stemmed from a casual acquaintance while he'd advised Oscar Bauer on diversifying his stock portfolio. The more money he'd made the respected land developer, the more work it'd brought Qasim and the more opportunity he had to "run into" the man's exquisite daughter.

Conversation and laughter had flowed freely between them. They'd never actually dated, but often wound up together when they found themselves at the same event. In the process of what he'd been sure had been politeness on Vectra's part, possessiveness had reared its head for him. Those tendencies had settled in hard and fast.

He'd come to expect her company at the functions they attended. He'd keep her on his arm or within reaching distance for the duration of the event. She never seemed to mind. She was the sweetest, loveliest thing he had ever seen, but she saw him as only a friend — one of many.

She had been confused by his behavior. It was best since he obviously couldn't rein in the stupid actions his sense of entitlement had driven him to. The way he'd behaved with Lewis Olin was proof enough of that.

Qasim muttered something foul, wishing he could kick his own ass for threatening the poor guy for simply picking up the phone to call her. She deserved an explanation, but he had no idea how to give her one now.

Oliver had been concerned when they'd gotten together for drinks several months prior. Vectra wasn't of a mind to totally abandon her shell, and Oliver couldn't gauge why after so long. He'd come to discuss it with Qasim. The two of them had become fast friends while Qasim had been reorganizing Oscar Bauer's financial portfolio.

The two bottles of whiskey they'd gone through that night had loosened tongues and pickled their brains, but not so much that Qasim forgot the pain he heard in the other man's voice as he shared his concern for his sister. Oliver was concerned that Vectra was still not venturing out on the dating scene.

Clearly, she wanted to enjoy herself, given

the number of invitations she accepted. Despite the parties she'd attended and traveling she'd done, Oliver and his father could tell she was hiding, and she was too special to lock herself away.

Qasim fully agreed. He'd resisted the urge to ask out the heiress, not wanting his interest in her to complicate his business relationship with her father. The time he'd spent getting to know Vectra, however, was making that less and less of a repellant.

Then, Oliver's loose tongue let slip an enraged curse upon the man who had "done that" to her. Qasim remembered both thanking and cursing his high tolerance for alcohol that night. Had he been more intoxicated, he may have forgotten Oliver telling him that his sister's last relationship had damn near destroyed her. The man she'd given her heart to had chosen to reciprocate her love with his abuse.

Whatever buzz he may've had from the whiskey had ceased and was then absorbed by the wave of rage. He'd only gotten a last name out of Oliver before the man passed out. Thankfully, it wasn't a last name Qasim recognized.

He knew enough, though. Not subjecting Vectra to his possessiveness became even more important after that revelation. He never wanted her to be afraid of him. He knew how much more of a possibility that could be if he let her see how little control he had over it.

He'd already blown it enough by threatening Lew. She was sure to shun him if he were to break some guy's nose just for shaking her hand. Besides, he'd heard the stories of how a man's possessiveness could be mistaken for love and the results it could bring. He wouldn't subject Vectra to that.

A calmer, more rational part of his soul called out that he wasn't that kind of man. Qasim discarded that as rubbish when he felt heat rush the back of his neck. Austin Sharpe, his arm still too snug about Vectra's waist, was escorting her from the dining room.

"Image is everything. You know that."

Vectra laughed while Austin relayed his lofty plans for her Miami gallery in collaboration with the event he wanted to hold.

"I've already had a thing on a yacht, but a gallery event would give me a chance to show off a different kind of style."

"Is that the same thing as image?" she teased.

Austin spread his hands accommodatingly. "Of course."

Vectra laughed, bracing a hand to his chest to steady herself.

"Vectra," Qasim called, voice flat and deep across the lobby, drawing her and Austin's attention.

"Sim." Austin smiled.

Qasim didn't spare the man a glance. "You done eating with your father?" he asked her.

"Well, I needed —" She stopped when he took her elbow, easing her out of Austin's grasp. Vectra cast a surprised look over her shoulder to Austin and found that he seemed more amused than confused or angry.

He waved. "We'll talk later, Vec. I need to get goin', anyway. Catch up with you later, Sim."

Vectra didn't check to see if Qasim had acknowledged Austin with a look or nod. He was taking her back into the dining room.

"What are you doing?" she whispered, practically able to feel the heat radiating off him in angry waves.

"Who are you going to Robb's party with, Vectra?"

The question caused her to stumble a bit. "Are you serious? Qasim, we need to talk."

"We have."

Vectra didn't realize they'd already returned to the table until Qasim helped her back into her seat.

"Join us, Qasim," Oscar Bauer offered.

Qasim's hand lingered on the back of Vectra's chair. "Maybe another time, sir." He didn't glance her way before he turned and left the dining room.

Chapter 4

Vectra accepted her brother's hand when he helped her down from his Jeep that evening. By that time, she'd almost forgotten how utterly bewildered she'd been early that morning.

"Good?" Oliver gave both her hands a shake when she stood before him on the sidewalk outside Dazzles. The restaurant-nightclub was owned by the party's guest of honor, Robb DeWitt.

"I promise I'm good." She eased a hand through the crook of his arm and squeezed. "Just please don't abandon me the second we walk up in here. I need to get my balance on these heels first."

Oliver's laughter turned heads almost as much as Vectra's dress. She was determined to enjoy herself. The little wiggle of anticipation haunting her spine was exciting, albeit annoying.

Vectra's gown was fashioned from a shimmering, elegant material — a cross between silk and satin. She hadn't known which, only that she loved it. Silver and turquoise ties secured the halter bodice that dipped scandalously low to the small of her bare back. The cool turquoise color was offset by the silver and turquoise folds of the skirt that flared elegantly about her ankles. Strappy silver heels peeked out to show off a fresh French pedicure.

She'd selected her dress with Qasim in mind even though her chances of seeing him were slim to none.

What the heck, she thought, smiling up and around at the energetic atmosphere.

She'd always enjoyed playing the odds whether or not they were in her favor.

Brother and sister spent the first ten to fifteen minutes greeting other guests they knew but parted ways soon after. Vectra had spotted someone she knew, and Oliver had no shortage of female acquaintances ready to pull him away with them.

Vectra laughed while hugging Derionte Weeks, the head chef for Dazzles.

"What are you doing out here when there are people to be fed?" she teased.

"I'm no fool, Vec. This is a self-service party." He grinned, looking quite pleased with himself. "The buffet is up on the VIP level."

"Smart man." Vectra arched a brow.

Derionte shrugged. "We're actually testing out some dishes to see which'll make the cut for Qasim's charity thing coming up."

"That's right." Vectra had almost forgotten the Dazzles cook staff had a standing job to work the highly anticipated event. "All that business is gonna earn you guys more than a few enemies."

Derionte rolled his eyes. "Look who's talkin'. The standing wine order comes from none other than Carro's."

"Hey, I can't help it if your boss has a weakness for the best," Vectra reasoned.

The music tempo changed and the two laughing friends immediately began to dance in place, syncing their moves to the upbeat nineties single.

Vectra and Derionte weren't out of place. Most of the people in the room had broken out into dance whether they were on the dance floor or not. The single had always been one of Vectra's favorites. She tossed her arms above her head, winding her hips as the grooves had their way with her body. She lost herself in the tune and didn't begrudge the pair of hands that had come up to steady her waist.

Smiling and happy to greet another dance partner, Vectra turned. She barely avoided stumbling when she saw that it was Qasim who had come up behind her. The song faded into another upbeat but more mellow single. It was another favorite, but suddenly Vectra wasn't in the mood for dancing. Her heart was beating way too fast to allow such activity.

"Sim." Derionte greeted Qasim, who side-stepped Vectra to give the man a hug and handshake. "I was just telling Ms. Bauer here that Carro's wine was on tap for your charity event."

Qasim returned his hands to Vectra's waist, deliberately smoothing them across her hips. "I hope that made Ms. Bauer happy."

"Continued business is always good." Vectra put on an easy expression for Derionte and tried to keep her mind off the way Qasim kept her back to his chest.

"We should set up a tasting to decide what'd go best with my menu. Are your folks out there workin' on any new blends, Vec?" Derionte queried.

"Always." She rested a hand against his forearm. "We should discuss it with your

60

boss. I haven't even told him happy birthday yet."

"He's up in the VIP level." Derionte chuckled. "Says he's gonna wait 'til a little later to make his appearance."

Qasim and Vectra groaned playfully over their old friend's penchant for grand entrances.

"Derry!" A petite waitress in a tuxedo-styled serving dress made her way through the crowd. "We need you in the kitchen."

Derionte rolled his eyes. "Duty calls. Hey, y'all go on up," he ordered, clapping Qasim's shoulder before he followed the waitress back through the robust crowd.

Vectra dropped her easy expression and turned a scathing glare upon Qasim.

"Who'd you come here with?" He took the lead of the conversation.

Vectra stepped back, disengaging his loose hold on her hip. "Are you prepared to answer the same question?"

He frowned. "What?"

"Please. Are you really that clueless? Or are you just trying to play dumb? Because you're pitiful at it if you are."

Qasim blinked, understanding pooling in his gaze as if something had clicked. "You think I brought someone here with me?"

"Didn't you?"

"No."

"Then what the hell is going on with you?" Whatever reservations she'd had vanished as her curiosity took hold. "Why would you say you don't want to be friends anymore? Did I say something? Do something wrong —" She grew quiet when he caught her elbow in a firm, yet remarkably gentle grasp and pulled her away from the crowd.

Vectra held on to Qasim's arm so she wouldn't stumble on her chic, yet outrageously high heels. Qasim didn't stop moving until he'd found an unoccupied remote section of the terrace. The structure ran the entire rear of Dazzles and overlooked the garden dining room below.

His hands smoothed up from her elbow to cup her slender neck, practically covering the entire column beneath a wide palm. His fingers played in the short crop of her blue-black hair where it tapered at her nape. His thumb tilted her chin up and back, studying the expression haunting her lovely face.

"Don't be afraid of me, Vec. Don't be afraid of me . . ." he whispered. The repeated words were silenced when his tongue outlined her mouth.

"Don't be afraid of me," he groaned, then took total possession of her mouth, backing her toward a remote corner of the terrace as he did so.

The contact was deep, seeking as he journeyed. He'd wanted her for so long and wasn't about to be cheated from a second's exploration.

Qasim invaded whatever personal space that existed between them as thoroughly as he invaded the sweet darkness beyond her lush lips. As close as he stood, he kept a hand at her hip, securing her against the smoothly finished wall at her back. He needed control — every ounce he could take. He knew that allowing her to be in charge of how close she got to him would very quickly get her stripped of a few choice articles of clothing as he helped himself to everything he needed from her.

Her tongue battled and engaged his as though it had a life of its own. Still, it took some time for Vectra to truly register that he was kissing her. She'd wanted it, had fantasized about it more times than she cared to admit — had pleasured herself over the way she'd imagined the experience. None of that even breached how wondrously shattering it was in reality.

God, but the man could kiss. He kept a hand firm at her hip when she so desperately wanted to seal herself against him. She had no complaints, however, about what she was being given leave to enjoy. He'd exchanged the ravenous intensity behind his lusty kisses for a more languid invasion.

Vectra reciprocated, winding her tongue slowly about his and then following up with an even more maddening suckle. Her heart, already lodged in the back of her throat, managed to flip when the sound of his whimper reached her ears.

He relaxed into her then, setting her more securely against the smooth wall. It was Vectra who nearly whimpered then. She steadied the movement of her lips, but her fingers frantically roamed his back through the crisp dark material of his shirt. As nice as the fabric felt beneath her fingers, she wanted him out of it.

Such was not to be, it seemed. Her fingers skimmed the buttons of the shirt. She wanted it parted and revealing the chest that felt like a slab of chiseled magnificence under her palms. She had but a few seconds to absorb the pleasure of the unyielding surface before he imprisoned both her wrists in his hand.

Qasim had just as much difficulty policing himself from snagging loose the ties that secured the halter bodice of her dress. He didn't dare lower his hands. One touch of her bare back would be his undoing. It was hard enough shackling her hands when all he wanted was to run his own across the flawless beauty of her caramel-toned skin.

He ended the kiss, but he couldn't resist another taste, beckoned by the sight of the pink tip of her tongue just visible beneath her sensually bruised lips.

Vectra arched into him, circling her arms about his neck. The groan he uttered rumbled as though it were somehow ampli-fied. He couldn't avoid skimming her bare back then.

Previous innocent touches to her arms, the back of her neck or a kiss to the cheek had already hinted at her softness. Having the opportunity now to actually massage her back, uncovered for his touch, drove the fact home. She was like satin in his hands. He whimpered again — no shame, all need.

Let her go, Sim. She's not for you.

The soft yet stinging reminder was enough to still the indulgent roaming of his hands even as his fingertips skimmed the lace scrap of the G-string panties she wore beneath the dress.

He broke the kiss suddenly and before he took her against the wall the way every last one of his hormones demanded him to. He dropped a brief kiss to her ear and let his mouth linger there.

"You haven't done anything wrong — not one thing." He gave her space, just a little. "Dance with me?" He silenced whatever precautions his voices of reason were giving him.

The music tempo had wound down to slow and sensual by the time Qasim and Vectra returned to the party room. The guest of honor and establishment's owner, Robb DeWitt, had not yet made his entrance. Spotlights flashed around a majestic ice-blue armchair near the front of the room in anticipation of the man's arrival.

Vectra was pleased by the distracting lights, which kept her and Qasim's sudden return below the radar. They wouldn't have garnered much attention anyway, she reasoned. They could usually be found together at some point during an event they both attended.

Qasim eased his hands about her waist, his thumbs drawing small circles where they touched her bare back.

Vectra exhaled on a long breath while linking an arm about Qasim's neck. She kept the other loosely linked about his side.

"Who brought you here?" he asked when

they'd been swaying to a slow, jazzy tune for the better part of three minutes.

Vectra had been enjoying the feel of whiskers along his jaw. They felt like mink next to her cheek. His question urged her, reluctantly, to raise her head.

"Oliver." Her gaze narrowed, watching him nod and give in to a faint, satisfied smile. "You approve? Why?"

"I just do."

"And that's it? I'm just supposed to accept that?"

"It's best if you did."

"Are you married?"

His very attractive features softened in amused shock. "You know I'm not married, Vectra." He laughed a bit.

"You're right, I do. Then the only reason I could see you approving of me coming to a party with my brother is because you're one of those guys who buys into that I-don't-want-you-but-no-one-else-can-have-you thing. Is that it?"

His amusement vanished. "I'm one of those guys who have a possessive streak."

Vectra blinked. "Possessive?" Her fingers dug into his shirt a little. "Over me? Why?"

Qasim kept one hand at Vectra's waist while the other lifted to massage her neck. "What was that you said to me about playing dumb? That I was pitiful at it? So are you."

Disbelief sparkled in her smoky gaze as she settled both hands to his chest and peered into his hooded stare. "We've been friends for so long —"

"And it's been hell, Vec."

His words stung, and she eased back as far as he'd let her. "I'm sorry."

"Babe —" he rested his forehead against hers "— you have nothing to be sorry for. I meant what I said out there. You haven't done anything wrong. This is my issue, and I won't see you hurt by it."

She curved her fingers into his shirt, a bit deeper that time. "You won't hurt me."

"I'd die first," he swore, cupping her face and gently squeezing where he held her. "You don't need someone as volatile as me in your life."

"But you want me."

Her simple observation had the potential to weaken every part of him.

"You're right. I do," he admitted with a shrug and a grin. "You've got no idea how much."

The sensual saxophone piece had segued into another instrumental selection, equally moving and romantic.

"You can have me. I want the same," she

said directly against his ear.

Stroking his knuckles across her jaw, Qasim felt himself teetering dangerously close to the verge of total weakness. "You're sweet with no idea of what you're saying to me."

She pulled her hand from his face. "I may be sweet, but I'm no innocent, Qasim. We're not involved with anyone else. We've been friends —"

"And I wish we could be just that, but I want you in my bed too damn bad. That's evident, isn't it?"

It was. The added inches her heels provided put them eye to eye, chest to chest, hip to hip. The impressive proof of his words was a thick, lengthy ridge against her thigh.

"I'm not complaining," her voice carried on scarcely a breath; it was that faint.

"Babe, you don't understand."

Confusion claimed her expression. "Then explain it to me. Are you afraid I'll become clingy? I can assure you I'm not a clingy woman."

Again, laughter softened the excellent craftsmanship of his face. "No, Vec, I'm not afraid of that." A man would have to be brain-dead not to want Vectra Bauer *clinging* to him.

"I'm not looking for an involvement,

Qasim." Her face changed, something haunted claiming it that time. "I've had enough of the committed-relationship game to last me a lifetime."

Qasim averted his head, hiding the sinful flex of a jaw muscle when he heard her outlook.

Applause interrupted their budding conversation as the guest of honor was announced. Qasim and Vectra turned to follow the direction of the spotlight trained on the wide stairway leading down from the establishment's VIP area. Robb DeWitt was finally making his entrance.

Vectra eased her clapping to finger a tear from her eye. She was sure the reaction hadn't been brought on by happiness, but frustration. Whatever the reason, she couldn't make herself resist Qasim's touch. He'd pulled her back to relax next to his chest to watch as their friend greeted his guests.

CHAPTER 5

"When are you gonna marry that beauty, Sim?" Robb DeWitt's sparkling hazel stare held challenge and amusement as he looked from Qasim to Vectra, who stood across the room.

Qasim shook his head. "I'd drive her crazy inside of a week."

"Ha! You know more about married life than you realize." Robb chuckled. "If you're not driving each other crazy by the first week, you're doing something wrong."

There was more laughter between the friends. Qasim sobered first.

"She doesn't know what she'd be getting into with me."

"Mmm . . . Army stuff?" Robb queried.

Qasim settled deeper into the armchair he occupied near Robb's spot at the front of the room. Additional chairs had been arranged in a semicircle around the man's towering royal blue chair to give the air of a king meeting his subjects.

Qasim massaged his eyes, considering his response to Robb's question. "Not in the way you mean, but it um . . . it plays a role."

"Ahh . . . and you don't think she could understand it?"

"Hmph, I'm not sure *I* even understand it, Robb."

"But you guys are here together —"

"We didn't come together."

Robb nodded, his expression smug. "Well, judging from what Davia saw on the dance floor, it looks like you'll be leaving together."

Qasim broke into soft laughter. "Does that woman miss anything?"

Robb looked over at his wife, who was chatting with Vectra. "She doesn't miss much, especially when it's so hard to miss."

"She's not for me," Qasim repeated, the words fast becoming his personal slogan.

"Do you realize that you're probably only one of a few men in this place who thinks that?"

Qasim propped his fist beneath his jaw and studied Vectra talking on the other side of the dining room. "She's an angel, Robb. She doesn't need a man who can't control his temper when it comes to the way other men behave around her."

"Agreed!" Robb laughed so hard he had

to thumb a tear from his eye. "I heard about your orders that no one else ask her to my party."

"Lew . . ." Qasim groaned. "Is there anybody he hasn't told about that?"

"In Lew's defense, he was probably talking about it out of sheer surprise rather than his obsession with honesty."

"I'm just predisposed to getting physical, I guess." Qasim shared the insight airily, but inside, the words stung.

Joining the military hadn't actually been his plan; his then financial situation had been a deciding factor. Additionally, he had viewed the military as a place that would welcome a guy who didn't mind shedding blood or having his own shed. He'd joined right out of high school and found more than his fill of violence and testosterone-driven angst.

He'd chosen not to make a career of it, however. Instead, he'd opted to complete his education on the government's dime. Money, not violence, had been his motivation and the only way to truly distance himself from an impoverished past. Still, all the degrees, money and respect in the world couldn't stifle his true nature — one he'd never regretted until Vectra Bauer came into his life.

"She doesn't seem like the type to get off on seeing guys come to blows over her," Robb noted.

"She's not and that's why I backed off our friendship." Qasim shrugged.

Robb laughed. "Backed off with conditions."

Qasim conceded the fact with another shrug. "It was wrong. I was threatening Lew before I knew what I was doing. I wouldn't have hurt him."

"So is backing away from Vec really necessary?"

A server stopped by the "king's court" with fresh drinks before Sim could respond.

"I enjoyed my tour in the army," he admitted, following a sip of the smooth bourbon. "I think I got addicted to the nonstop adrenaline. I craved it more than anything."

"And the killing?" Robb kept his gaze fixed down into the stout, beaded glass he held. "Were you addicted to that, too?"

Qasim didn't need to think about that, and the answer was quick and genuine. "No, not the killing." He twisted his glass, swirling the liquid there. "But I'd be lying if I told you I didn't get a certain amount of enjoyment off the power."

He set aside his glass. "Knowing I held someone's life in my hands. That I had the authority and approval from others to take it . . . made it difficult for me not to find satisfaction over it. That's why I didn't make a career of it. The way I felt about what I was expected to do over there . . . scared me."

Robb raised his glass in toast. "And now you've got more power than you know what to do with."

Qasim reached for his glass, reciprocating the toast. "Making money is the best kind of therapy."

"A woman's love and affection can be an even better kind."

"Robb . . ." Qasim rested his head against the high back of the chair. "I might agree with you if all this possessive crap hadn't reared its ugly head again the second I admitted to myself how much I want her in my bed."

"You promised not to do this to me, Olive."

"Are you really gonna try to convince me that no one else here could give you a ride home?"

Vectra smiled tightly. "I can see you haven't learned much about wooing women from your father. Taking your date back home is one of the top rules."

"But we're talking about *you,* not

women."

Vectra attacked Oliver's shoulder with a playful yet firm punch. They both dissolved into full-blown laughter over the tease and the action that followed.

"Look, Vecs, all the men here are guys I trust." Oliver planted a fist to the center of his chest. "I even took the liberty of asking one."

Vectra followed her brother's gaze past her shoulder to where Qasim approached them from the curving hallway that led to an outer balcony along the VIP room.

"Olive," Vectra spoke through clenched teeth.

Oliver kept his voice low. "Don't even try it. I caught your dance earlier. What was going on when you disappeared before that?" He moved on to greet Qasim with a handshake and hug before Vectra could lash out with her retort.

She kept her palms plastered at her sides to resist fisting them. She and Qasim had parted ways shortly after bestowing warm birthday greetings upon Robb DeWitt.

Qasim had stopped to talk with Robb for a while and she'd taken time to chat with Robb's wife, Davia. Afterwards, Vectra had mingled a bit more until she'd caught up with Oliver only to have her brother tell her he'd made plans to spend the rest of the evening with one of his female acquaintances.

"I hope taking her home won't put you out too much," Oliver said. "I could easily toss her butt in a cab."

Qasim grinned broadly at the man's merciless teasing. "It's no problem." He waved toward Vectra. "You ready?"

"More than," she gritted, elbowing her brother out of her way as she moved past him.

"Have a good night." Oliver sent a wink in Qasim's direction.

Qasim jogged a little to catch up to Vectra. She'd bolted off, taking the back exit from the VIP balcony that led down into the garden dining area. It was a lush spot smack-dab in the middle of stately trees and vibrant flora that lent splashes of dazzling color, hence Robb DeWitt's motivation in naming his establishment Dazzles.

Vectra had taken a seat on one of the wrought-iron benches along the man-made pond that wound through the dining area. There, she had removed her shoes to massage her dance-weary feet. The black benches were accentuated with coral-colored cushions to encourage patrons to relax there in greater comfort. Vectra was securing the strap of a sandal when Qasim sat down next to her. He watched her intently — fascination pooling in his stare as it fixed on the sandal cupping her delicate foot and the thin ties about a trim ankle.

She paused before putting on the next sandal, taking time to rub her arch, using her thumb to work the muscle there.

The look of utter delight upon her lovely features held Qasim entranced. Her eyes were closed, and he thought it must be the way she appeared when she slept. He couldn't imagine himself ever wanting to let her out of his bed if it was.

The interlude ended far too soon for his liking. Vectra finished securing the second sandal and Qasim found himself tilting his head to follow the trail of her leg bared by the raised hem of her dress. The curve of her thigh had him rubbing and squeezing his hands in hopes of quelling the desire to feel the lush limb beneath his palm.

"Ready." She stood.

"You have a bag? Wrap?" He stood, dark gaze wandering adoringly across her bare arms and shoulders.

"Too warm for a wrap and I've got everything else I need here."

Qasim watched as she patted a spot along her upper thigh. At his confusion, Vectra smirked and took his hand. She repeated the patting move, this time guiding his hand along her thigh. There was an uneven spot.

"It's a pouch for my ID and money . . ."

Qasim was reluctant to move his hand when Vectra released it but made himself ease back.

"Most women need to carry more than that," he observed.

"Most, maybe, but not all," Vectra explained with a cool smile. "I wasn't planning on going anywhere but the party and back home. I keep a house key hidden someplace inconspicuous, and security at the estate is amazing so I don't see the need to bog myself down with a bag."

"Makeup?" he inquired, in awe of her without realizing just how much.

Vectra brushed the back of one hand across a flawless cheek. "Only lipstick — a brand I love because so far it's living up to its claims of withstanding anything from a multicourse meal to a full-blown . . . kiss." She realized where her rambling had taken her and cleared her throat while observing Qasim's steady gaze.

"I'm ready," she said, managing a tiny smile when he offered his arm.

"I really can get myself home," she told him once they'd fallen into step.

"And that'd be fine if I weren't here to take you myself. I promise you'll enjoy my driving."

Vectra swallowed, wondering why it was so easy for her to attach sexual overtones to almost everything the man said.

Vectra didn't know if it was Qasim's skill behind the wheel or the hypnotic purr of the Sequoia's engine that made her eyes heavy with relaxation. They'd set out for Saint Helena. Qasim continued their listening enjoyment of the nineties' jams going with the satellite station tuned and at a volume that was just loud enough to make talking unnecessary.

Lack of conversation, though, only heightened the desire to indulge in a nap. Vectra didn't slumber deeply and was waking when Qasim pulled to a halt in the Y-shaped dirt drive before the gorgeous brick mansion where she'd lived most of her life.

The secluded oasis was tucked within the picturesque scenery of the Carro Vineyards. The stunning beauty of the unbelievable mountain views in the distance was evident even outlined against the night sky.

Vectra needed a moment to find her bearings, but Qasim was already out of the vehicle by the time she'd turned to thank him for the ride home.

"Thanks." She accepted his help down from the SUV step bar.

"Welcome." He waved a hand, directing her to precede him to the front door.

"What are you doing?"

"What does it look like?"

"Qasim —"

"You've got questions. I'd like to answer them, Vec."

She wasted no more time and went to an obscenely big potted fern that rested on a tall, large base. Qasim watched her stoop before the brick column and wiggle a loose brick free. From the space it left, she retrieved a key.

"Inconspicuous, huh?" he chided.

"And amazing security," she reminded him.

Qasim bit his tongue, stifling the urge to tell her that amazing security was no excuse for carelessness. The main house at Carro Vineyards was a vast construction possessing an open floor plan that played to its natural environment. The place had been erected almost dead center of the healthy crops, so views of the coveted vineyards met the eye from every direction.

As exquisite as the place was, Qasim

81

wasn't overly fond of all the bay windows. They provided an onlooker with an unobstructed view of the home's interior, which was a warm, beckoning sight thanks to the golden light that filled all the rooms on the lower level.

He didn't like the idea of just anyone being able to peer in on Vectra when she was there alone.

"Where's your staff?"

"Oh, they always have the weekends off unless there's some event in progress. In that case, we have a skeleton crew on board. That's all I was able to get Dad to go for when he hired this staff I don't need."

"Are you serious? You mean you'd try shutting off *all* these lights by yourself?"

She laughed. "It wouldn't be a problem. The lights are timed to engage at night and shut off at dawn."

"I see." Qasim peered through the entrance. "And are your windows open this way all over the house?"

"No, I keep it darker up there." She pointed upward, smiling at the way he studied the high ceilings after they entered the house.

They then ventured beyond the brick-and-stone foyer and into the attached library.

"Haven't you seen the entire house?" A

dubious frown claimed her face when Qasim shook his head.

"My meetings with your father usually took place at his condo in the city." He kept his gaze fixed on the high beams and recessed lighting. "The few times I met him here with Oliver, we kept to the patios or had a meal set up in the vineyard. I've only been inside a few times."

Vectra smiled in understanding. Despite their budding friendship, there had never been occasion to bring him there. She guessed they were actually more along the lines of close acquaintances than friends. A friend would have some idea of what the inside of their friend's home looked like, right?

She dismissed the idea, deciding whatever "answers" she wanted from Qasim could wait at least until she'd given him a tour. She took a seat on a settee nearest the library entrance.

"I hope your shoes are comfortable," she warned him while slipping out of her sandals for the second and final time that night.

At the party, she'd finally taken to socializing from a comfy spot in the Dazzles dining room. There, she'd removed her shoes after having had her fill of the chic heels.

"So have you seen the library?" she asked him.

"I know the lower level."

Nodding, Vectra pushed to her feet. "Two more floors to go, then. Follow me."

Qasim felt much better about the elaborate and way too "open" home by the end of Vectra's impromptu tour. The upper level was where her office, a second den and an astonishing pool room were located. Guest rooms and a bar occupied that floor, as well.

The second floor actually branched off into a third level that only housed Vectra's master bedroom suite and a sumptuous spa and hot tub area.

"And I thought I'd reached the top with my place at Sea Cliff." He grinned, realizing Vectra had overheard him and started to laugh.

"My folks didn't buy it like this." She looked up and around, as well. "If you can believe it, the property was nothing but acres and acres of uncultivated land when they came here as newlyweds. They added on to the place brick by brick the more successful they got with the vineyard."

Qasim's gaze softened. "I can tell you're proud of them."

"They're easy to be proud of." Vectra's

cocoa-rich stare took on a faraway look. "Everyone should have parents that great."

"You're right."

He'd agreed, but Vectra could tell that his heart wasn't totally in it. She figured there was an unhappy story there, but she decided that it wasn't the time to pry. "You said something about giving me answers?"

Qasim appreciated the subject change, though he'd expected them to return to the lower level first. The tour had ended in the entertainment parlor outside her bedroom suite.

Vectra didn't believe she'd consciously ended things there on purpose. *Sub*consciously . . . She wouldn't bet on it. Given how heated things had been between them earlier that night, serious discussion in the bedroom was perhaps not the best idea.

So be it, Vectra thought.

She got comfortable in the spot she'd selected on a wide chair upholstered in a print of violet, coral and hunter-green flora. The chair flanked an overstuffed sofa fashioned with recliners on either end of the U-shaped piece.

"Why can't we be friends, Qasim?"

"I told you why. I want you in bed."

"And wanting me in bed is a problem

because . . ."

He began to walk the room, gradually pleased by her decision to talk there. It had a calming effect. An area rug covered gleaming hardwood and carried the same designs as the chair she occupied. The paint adorning the walls had a grainy texture, and the color was a mix of the same tones woven into the rug and furniture upholstery. The combination was sponged upon the walls and gave the image of a sky at sunset.

"Do you remember me telling you I was in the army?" He watched her nod.

"I went in right after high school, stayed until my midtwenties, started my business while I was in college afterwards."

He smiled in a manner Vectra thought was adorably bashful.

"I have a talent for getting people to trust me with their money," he added.

Vectra tugged her legs beneath her on the chair. "It's a good thing you also have a talent for making them more of it."

Qasim replied with only a half smile. "In the army, people trusted me to kill, and I had a talent for that, too."

She blinked, a somberness filtering her wide, entrancing eyes. "And this is why you don't want me in your bed? Because you

86

enjoyed your army obligations a little too much?"

"Part of what led me to the army is still very much a part of who I am. I don't have an insatiable urge to kill, but I believe deep down I'm still more prone to violence than I should be."

She leaned forward. "You wouldn't hurt me."

"You don't know me, Vectra."

"Because you won't let me."

"Vectra, a guy like me . . . the kind of guy I have the potential to be . . . you don't need that. Not after what you've had to deal with."

Vectra shrank back, blinked. Reluctant understanding nudged aside the somberness in her gaze. "How do you know that?" Slowly, she shook her head. "You . . . you can't know that . . ."

Qasim crossed to her, shredding the distance between them in that stealthy manner of his. He reached down, fingering the clipped strands of her hair before cradling her elegant jaw in his wide palm.

"I know it, honey. I know it."

She expelled a puff of breath, blinking rapidly as though she were attempting to swat away the truth. She didn't want to sit anymore and left the chair only to stumble and claim a spot on the sofa. Deep cold penetrated her bones, causing her entire body to tremble. She looked at Qasim. Disbelief coursed her veins motivated by the knowledge that he knew about her the very last thing she ever wanted him to.

Qasim went to his knees beside the sofa where Vectra sat, but she extended a hand to urge him to keep his distance.

"How? How do you . . ." She kept her face turned away from him. Tears hadn't left the cradle of her eyes; they had merely pooled there. She swore that was all they would do. Never again would she cry over the weakness she'd once given freedom to rule her.

"Who told you?" She approved of the strength she heard in her voice.

Qasim toyed with the silken fabric of her flaring skirt. "I had drinks with Oliver a while back."

Tears fell then out of anguish instead of self-pity. With an enraged cry, Vectra bolted from her place on the sofa.

"Oliver . . . damn you . . ." she whispered.

Regretting his honesty, Qasim drew a fist, which he slammed upon the vacated couch. Vectra had moved across the room, appearing to study a waterscape portrait on the wall. He read her profile and surmised that she wasn't really seeing the artwork.

"In Oliver's defense, I doubt he remembers saying anything to me." Qasim sat in the chair, leaning forward and bracing elbows to knees. "We got pretty drunk that night."

"How'd my name even come up?" Her voice was thick around the sob lodged in her throat.

"We'd finished talking business." Qasim shrugged, a wry smile defining his lush mouth. "I asked how you were doing. Oliver couldn't hide his concern, told me he and your father wanted you to stop locking yourself away." Qasim sighed, massaging his eyes in an attempt to hide the rage stirring there. "He said that in spite of your friends and the gallery, romantic involvement was something you still shied away from. He said he knew it was because of that jackass who 'touched you' was the way he put it."

The eye massage hadn't helped. Qasim fought to quell rising temper over what Oliver Bauer had confessed to him.

"Once I heard that, I kept the liquor flowing until he told me everything. Your brother's tolerance level is nowhere near mine." Qasim studied the life lines in his palm, tracing them with his thumb. "I, um . . . I wasn't proud of getting him so sauced, but I had to know. Oliver spent the night at my place. We had breakfast the next morning. He didn't seem to remember telling me anything."

"My dad and Olive were the only ones who knew." Vectra turned away from the painting she'd half studied. "I don't want anyone's pity, Qasim."

He straightened in the chair. "I don't pity you, Vectra."

"But you *do* think I'm too fragile to have a man in my bed."

"No, I think you're too fragile to have *me* in your bed."

She smiled. "FYI, you're tempting me more than discouraging me."

He reclined in the chair, rubbing at his jaw while he regarded her. "Threatening Lew came out of nowhere. You deserve better than to have another guy in your bed that wants to half kill a man every time one looks at you."

Vectra moved, her steps carrying her within inches of where Qasim relaxed in her favorite chair. She reached out, nails grazing his whisker-shaded jaw before she toyed with the open collar of his shirt.

"*Wanting* to half kill a man is a lot different than actually following through on it, and if you're gonna 'what if' every aspect of

90

our relationship before we actually have one, then I guess we didn't really have any business trying to get one started."

He stood. "Vectra —"

"You can show yourself out." She treated herself to a few more seconds of caressing the back of her hand across the mink-soft whiskers claiming his very gorgeous face. "The door will lock behind you when you go." Briefly, she rested her hand flat on his chest and mourned the fact that she wouldn't get to experience feeling what felt like sheer magnificence bare beneath her fingertips.

"Good night, Qasim." She moved past him to head into her bedroom, stopping just before she passed through the double doors.

"By the way, the only thing Keith was jealous or possessive of was my money, and he didn't like it much when I told him he couldn't have any more of it." Vectra moved into her room and let the doors close at her back.

CHAPTER 6

"Qasim?" Minka Gerald traded unsteady looks with the other people at the long, rectangular table that Monday morning. She resorted to leaning forward to tap Qasim's hand, smiling encouragingly when he focused on her face as if he had no idea what she was doing there.

"Do you need more time to decide?" she asked. "We've been giving this business to area hotels for years now. We all think this could be a good alternative." Her smile faltered a bit, and she glanced toward the opposite end of the conference table. "*Most* of us think it's a good alternative."

"Changing venues is a *big, complex* alternative," Will Lloyd stated.

"Changing venues?" Qasim's interest heightened a tad.

"This event requires lots of planning and detail." Will leaned forward in his chair. "A lot of that planning depends on the location. The hotels already have the necessary personnel in place to handle a lot of those details. Holding this thing at a private residence brings the brunt of that work way down on our shoulders.

"Given that *I'm* the one who has the job of planning this thing, I certainly don't want to be responsible for screwing up the first time we decide to shake up the status quo."

"This would save a lot of dollars from the bottom line." Minka's voice was flat, cool. "Dollars that could go to the donations side of the charity. It *is* why you started this, isn't it?"

"So what's the plan if we change venues?" Qasim asked.

Minka cast another look around the table. The group seemed fine with letting her step out on the ledge and answer the boss. "We thought Carro Vineyards would be the perfect location."

Qasim frowned, not bothering to hide his surprise over the suggestion.

Minka lifted her hands in a show of mock defense. "Don't shoot it down just yet. I got the idea when Vectra came to the office last week. We just want your permission to talk to her about it. I think we have an excellent chance at getting her blessings on the go-ahead.

"We all know that Carro holds that grape-gathering event every year for the kids. Having a part to play in something like this might be very exciting for them."

Qasim thought he could feel his nerves grating, but admitted his frugal assistant had a point. No one could argue the fact that the Bauer family had no qualms about giving back. The annual Grape Gathering had been established by Rose Bauer, and Vectra had done more than simply continue her late mother's charity extravaganza. It had been her idea to hold a special day exclusively for the very kids the proceeds from the Grape Gathering admission tickets were to benefit.

Local children from low-income families and those living in homeless shelters in and around the greater San Francisco area were invited out for a day of grape picking. The event began with a mountainous breakfast and continued with breaks for generous lunch and supper buffets.

"Think of the money we could save," Minka urged her boss. "Vectra probably wouldn't even charge us to hold the event there."

Qasim shifted on his seat at the head of the long table. Rubbing his eyes, he attempted to veil the doubt lurking there.

After the other night, the charitable mistress of Carro Vineyards might very well charge an arm and a leg for the privilege of hosting.

An arm and a leg is right — my own!

"We've got nothing to lose by asking," someone at the table said.

"I like the idea of having it at a vineyard instead of some stuffy old hotel," another agreed.

"Great idea, Mink," someone else cheered.

Will stood suddenly and began to collect his belongings. "You guys will have to excuse me. Good luck, Minka. Sim, do you want me to keep working on this, or should I turn the event back over to Minka? It's been her baby for a few years now." He tugged at his tie indignantly. "Maybe she wasn't as ready to give it up as you thought when you asked me to handle it."

"I don't think she's looking to have all that work back." Qasim attempted to play the role of peacemaker. It was very necessary for him to be fully committed to the conversation. Just then, however, he had no real interest in locales, budgets or any other aspects of the early-morning meeting.

After leaving Vectra's, following their heavy conversation, he'd told himself that it was for the best. It was what he'd wanted

95

after all, right? An involvement between them wasn't the best idea, was it?

"Nothing's set in stone, Will," he said, "but anything that puts more money into the hands of the kids I'm trying to help has to be worth checking out. We keep Minka pretty busy around here. I'm sure she's not trying to heap more work on her plate."

Minka waved a hand. "Definitely *not* trying to grab more work."

Will nodded stiffly. "Then I'll just wait to hear from you on when I can get back to my job."

The room was silent as everyone watched Will leave.

Qasim pushed back from the table. "If there's no more business, meeting adjourned. Minka? Stick around."

"So? Was I right?" he asked her when they were alone. "Do you really have enough on your plate, or is this your way of telling me you want back in on organizing the charity weekend?"

"I swear I have enough to keep me busy. I only got the idea after seeing Vectra the other day and then going over those hotel projections Will dropped off." Minka pushed at the edge of the legal pad before her on the table. "I just thought I'd be a better person to talk to her about it than Will."

"Agreed." Qasim left the table and went to pour himself a glass of cranberry juice from the bar cart.

Minka doodled on the pad while Qasim prepared his drink. "Can I ask you something?" She looked up, taking his silence as permission to continue. "Do you think Will's the best person for this job?"

"Concerns?" Qasim's interest in business was then very much back on track. He tilted back some of his juice and waited for Minka's response.

"No, only it takes a certain amount of patience and finesse to put these events together. Maybe Will would like something different but doesn't feel right asking after everything you've done for him already."

Qasim came back to the table, sat on its edge. "I thought giving him something far removed from what he was used to might be the way to go." He gave a skeptical smile. "You think I screwed up?"

Minka was quick to shake her head. "No, Will handled the job very well, in my opinion. Putting this event together isn't easy. Hopefully, he'll find his other responsibilities a breeze after this."

"Yeah . . . his responsibilities have a lot of people concerned . . . I've never seen anyone cooler under pressure, and he's been in some situations where 'cool under pressure' is a coveted skill," he tacked on, not meaning to reveal quite so much.

Minka didn't appear to notice her boss's slip. "Well, he was in the army, too." A smile illuminated Minka's round, pretty face. "That's where you guys met, right?"

The corner of Qasim's mouth tilted upward while he studied the contents of his glass. "Where we met — where he saved my life. When he came to me down on his luck . . . I felt like I owed him."

Minka held out her hands over the pad. "He saved your life, Sim. If that isn't a reason to give somebody a job, I don't know what is."

Qasim laughed while Minka stood to collect her things.

"I should go smooth things over with him," she said. "Do you think flowers would go over well?"

Qasim chuckled. "I know he likes Venus flytraps."

"Ha! Okay then, so that's a 'no' on the flowers." She tapped her pad to the table and shifted her weight. "So was there anything else?"

Qasim returned his juice glass to the bar. "Nope. We're good."

"You sure? I'm here if you want to discuss

anything else . . . like Vectra Bauer."

Turning, Qasim narrowed his gaze and waited.

Minka rolled her eyes. "It's obvious your head wasn't in that meeting."

"I'm good, Mink. Thanks for lending an ear."

"Anytime." Minka collected her things and left Qasim alone in the conference room.

Vectra swatted at the fuzz tickling her nose. It tickled something fierce, causing her to sneeze instead of laugh. The gesture awakened her, and she caught the source of her distress.

The sight of brown eyes, so similar to her shade but enhanced by a lighter hue that emphasized playful cunning, gazed back at her. At once, Vectra felt any anger she'd held for Oliver vanish. She pitied the woman her big brother finally set his sights on.

The girl is gonna have a hard time staying angry with this one, she thought.

At any rate, Oliver's adorable yet devilish persona didn't stop her from laying into him with blows from one of the pillows lining the cushioned headboard of her bed.

"You. Scared. Me. To. Death!" she cried,

syncing her words with the blows from the pillow.

He laughed, covering his head to shield the hits. "I swear that was a sneeze and not a scream I heard!"

Vectra landed one more blow for good measure and then collapsed. "Why are you here and not laid up with one of your many sex kittens?"

"There aren't that many." Oliver relaxed near the foot of her bed.

"Hmph." Vectra pursed her lips. "Does all that modesty keep your male friends from hating you?"

Oliver grinned. "It's not always a good idea to sleep over. It can send the wrong impression."

"Right." Vectra tossed another pillow in the man's direction. "You'll change your tune when the time and the woman are right."

"Well, the time wasn't right on Friday." Oliver plumped the pillow and placed it beneath his head. "I was preoccupied with wanting to come and check on you."

Vectra lifted her brows. "Ahh . . . not so faithful in your ride for me after all?"

"That's not it." Oliver threw up a wave. "Sim's a good guy, but I wanted to stop over and check on you, too."

"And what if Qasim and I had been . . . indisposed?"

Oliver snuggled his head deeper into the pillow. "I'd have knocked. Anyway, that's why I decided to wait — give you two the weekend."

"How sweet of you."

"It's the kind of guy I am."

Vectra tried to kick his shoulder, but he was too far away.

"There's coffee," he said. "Charlotte was leaving it when I got here. I guessed it was safe to come in."

Vectra noticed the cart that had been pushed into her bedroom and smiled. The surface would be laden with coffee *and* tea. While she was more of a tea drinker, there were mornings when her tastes called for something stronger than the herbal blends she adored.

"What'll you have?" Oliver pushed up from the bed.

Vectra kneaded the bunched muscles at her nape. "I think I need tea this morning."

"Hmm . . . Friday night too tension filled?"

Vectra shook her head over the man's blatant prying.

He noticed, shrugged. "Hey, I waited long enough. It *is* Monday, after all, and I was tired of waiting on you to call and yell at me for having Sim drive you home." He poured a mug of his preferred black, unsweetened coffee.

"I wouldn't have yelled." Vectra drew her knees up to her chin. "It's not every day a girl has Qasim Wilder drive her home."

"So I'm forgiven?"

"If you hurry up with my tea."

Oliver did as he was told. "This is progress," he said when handing her the tea. "Wasn't long ago when you would've lashed out at Dad or me something fierce for even hinting there was a guy we wanted to set you up with."

"Is that what you're trying to do?" Vectra blew across the surface of the tea. "Set me up with Qasim Wilder?"

"I'm worried about you, girl."

Vectra saw how serious he was. Carefully, so as not to drop her tea, she eased back on the bed and patted the space beside her. "I thought you'd be happy that I wasn't bringing home any more idiots."

Oliver gulped his coffee, apparently unaffected by its hot temperature. "You didn't exactly bring Keith Freedman home. Mom and Dad were responsible for that."

"Hear, hear." Vectra raised her mug in toast.

Technically, Oliver was correct. Keith Freedman's parents had been hired by Oscar and Rose to work as gardeners on Carro. Keith had started out as a childhood friend who'd turned into an adult nightmare for Vectra.

"We just don't like seeing you lock yourself away."

"It's easier."

Oliver bumped her shoulder with his. "Like my decision not to spend nights over. Easier."

Vectra smiled.

Oliver shrugged. "That is, until the time and the man are right."

She nodded once at his play on her words. "I'll be sure to let you know when that happens."

"Hasn't it already?"

She sipped at her tea, considering her response. "Qasim's only a friend. He's been one for a while, you know?"

"I know a lot about having female friends who are just friends, Vecs. I also know a lot about having female friends I want to take to bed. Sim Wilder doesn't look at you like a female friend who's just a friend."

Vectra dissolved into actual giggles, and she only gave in to them when she was around her big brother.

"Should you be telling me this? Aren't these playa secrets or something?"

Oliver shrugged. "Sim's a good guy."

"And you and Dad approve, is that it?"

"As far as me and Dad are concerned, nobody's good enough, but, yeah, we approve even though we know you don't give a damn."

"I approve, too." She wiggled her brows when Oliver looked stunned. "But it turns out Qasim isn't as interested as you think." She tapped out a morose tune against her mug. "He thinks he's too rough around the edges for me — seems pretty set on us not being more than what we are."

Oliver winced. "Hell, kid, I'm sorry." He looped an arm around her shoulders, tugged her close.

Vectra accepted the refuge of the embrace. "At least it ended before we made total fools of ourselves." She closed her eyes and tried to dismiss the fact that she may have done so for a chance with Qasim Wilder.

CHAPTER 7

Giving a struggling artist cause to celebrate made Vectra feel like celebrating, as well. A good thing, too, given her frame of mind lately. The artist, Yancey Croachman, created pieces that, to the naked eye, looked like mere splotches of paint dashed against the canvas in no discernible design.

A closer look, however, proved that there was, in fact, some method to the young British-Canadian's madness. Hidden in the wild splatters of paint were intricately designed portraits that, once spotted, took the observer's attention completely away from the more eye-catching explosions of color.

Vectra had been extremely optimistic about the showing after having enjoyed the hours she'd spent studying the artist's work. She'd been surprised each time she honed in on one of the hidden drawings.

Yancey and her agent brimmed with

excitement. The young artist had not yet gained a huge following in the States.

"A showing of scale is what my client needs," Yancey's agent, Cooper Perkins, said to Vectra. "My client on a respected stage like yours," he spread his hands. "She'll be the new darling of the art world."

Yancey caught Vectra's eyes amidst the man's rambling. Her expression told Vectra that she didn't buy into all that "new darling" stuff but that she was definitely over the moon about her first big showing at Vectra's well-known and respected Gallery V.

"Well, my staff and I like to give our artists the virtual run of the gallery." Vectra recrossed her legs at the booth table and leaned in a bit. "Short of knocking down walls and giving the place a new paint job, we'd like the spot to reflect more of who you are. Furniture, lighting, even music we leave to you. We'll set up time for you to discuss those things with our floor managers and see what you guys come up with."

Yancey's excitement went into overdrive and the petite redhead seemed to be on the verge of bursting.

Vectra laughed, taking both her hands. "Breathe. You've still got another showing at the Miami gallery after this one."

Yancey nodded firmly as though she were giving herself a silent pep talk. "I still can't believe this is happening."

"Believe it." Vectra gave her hands another shake. "I tell you what'll help is for you to go back to the hotel, relax and then get dolled up for a night on the town. Once you get deep into preparing for this show, you'll barely have time to brush your teeth — let alone go out for dinner."

Yancey laughed while Cooper Perkins voiced his agreement.

"We came here straight from the airport. We could use a few minutes of downtime," he said, reaching over to shake hands with Vectra. "Thank you, Ms. Bauer."

Yancey stood and rounded the table to hug Vectra. Soon after, agent and client left the dining room of the Italian grill where they'd met for lunch.

"Looks like you've made two people very happy."

Vectra turned, smiling even as a curious frown brought her brows close. She latched on to the name that floated highest in her memory. "Will?" She tapped a finger to her jaw and searched for the rest. "Lloyd?"

Will laughed. "You're good. Most people give me Smith instead of Lloyd."

Vectra laughed and shook hands with the

man she knew to be part of Qasim's staff. "How are you? Are you here on the clock or just to enjoy the food?"

Will shrugged. "Bit of both." He nodded toward the front of the dining room. "Looks like you were handling some happy business."

"Yeah, the showing." Vectra smiled toward the restaurant's entrance. "Fun part's giving the artist the news that the event is a go, and then all the real work begins. That part isn't so much fun."

"Guess it takes a lot to put those things together?"

Vectra shrugged, slapping her hands to the amber-colored toga dress that accentuated her caramel-toned legs. "I have a very good staff, so my workload is surprisingly light. You'd be surprised how fast they can put together a phenomenal show."

"Ms. Bauer? Will there be anything else?" her waiter asked.

"Join me for a drink?" Will asked before Vectra could reply. "There's something I'd like to run by you."

Intrigued, she smiled. "Sure." She gave the waiter a smile. "Royce, could you bring me another white wine?"

"No problem. And for you, sir?"

"Scotch. Dewar's," Will requested then

helped Vectra back into her seat and claimed the one opposite her.

"So?" she prompted when the waiter had gone to fill the orders.

"Vectra, you know about the charity event Sim holds every year for his scholarship kids, right?"

"Sure." She nodded. "I think it's great."

"It really is. We had a meeting about it today and unfortunately it looks like we're gonna have a few extreme issues."

"Yuck." She made a face. "Well, what kind of problems? That event's pretty popular. I can't imagine he'd have a problem finding someone to host it."

Will shook his head. "Lots of great people to host, but the money they want to do it takes dollars out of what we should be giving to charity."

It was Vectra's turn to shake her head. "Understood."

Will grunted a laugh. "Sim would pay all the expenses out of his own pocket, but no one wants him to do that. Besides, the charity brings in enough for everybody to be happy."

"True, but when it comes to charities, the more money you put in the hands of the people you want to help, the better."

"You're right." Will cradled a hand against

his cheek, considering. "Guess it wasn't such a bad plan after all." He noticed Vectra's curious frown and grinned.

"At the meeting, they tossed around the idea of having the event at your vineyard. I know it's a lot to ask given everything you already do for the community." Will shook his head, still grinning. "Sim didn't like the idea at all."

Vectra stiffened. "He had a problem with using my vineyard?"

"He didn't seem all that excited about it, but then neither was I when Minka suggested it." He shrugged. "That was probably just my own agitation thinkin' Minka was trying to take back her job."

The idea was actually quite appealing to Vectra. True, she had a lot of pots on the stove in regard to the many obligations, charitable and otherwise, that she was responsible for. Despite that, her family — her mother, especially — had instilled in her from a young age that it was the duty of those with more to assist those with less whenever they could.

As a result, Carro Vineyards was as widely known for producing fantastic wine as it was for seeing to the needs of the less fortunate. Besides, and Vectra could admit it being selfish reasoning on her part, it was a chance to do something Qasim wouldn't like. The fact that he'd let their personal differences interfere with doing what needed to be done for charity's sake set her teeth on edge.

The waiter returned with their drinks.

"So how'd the meeting end?" Vectra asked, sipping her wine. It wasn't a Carro blend, but it was delicious just the same.

"Well, Sim gave the go-ahead to run the idea by you, so . . ."

"That's terrific since I'm interested in hearing more. I'm sure this is an event Carro could host successfully."

Will nursed his drink, looking progressively uncertain. "The idea was really Minka's. She's the one who was supposed to discuss this with you, and since I'm the new kid on the block, I don't want to get on anyone's bad side. Especially hers."

Vectra laughed. "I don't see that being a problem. Especially with Minka. You said the job was yours now, so we'll keep everyone in the loop. Maybe a dinner meeting with you, Minka and whomever else needs to be in on it."

"Sounds good." Will nodded, the satisfaction returning to his gaze.

Vectra took another quick sip of her wine, glimpsed her watch and winced. "I should be going, Will. Listen, if you guys can work out a time and place to meet, call me with the details and it should be fine."

"Thanks, Vectra. I can see why Sim likes you."

"Thanks." She tried to mask a deep inhale over the observation. "You and Qasim go back pretty far, huh?"

"Pretty far, yeah . . ." Will's expression betrayed faint signs of something haunted. "I wish it'd been a friendship born out of want instead of necessity."

"That sounds ominous."

His smile was somber. "You can't get more ominous than the thick of battle."

"Right." Her eyes widened.

Will toyed with the rim of his glass. "Things got pretty hairy over there, but I got a good friend out of the hell of it."

"Your hell turned into the blessing of a good friend."

"That's truer than you know." Will's smile brightened. "My life was always hell. I thought going into the service couldn't make it any worse."

"Sounds like Qasim made it better. He's a great guy to know."

"You're right. Nothing much changed after the army. I was more down on my luck than ever. I reached out to Sim on a whim and the guy gave me a job I was nowhere near qualified for."

Vectra squeezed Will's arm beneath his suit coat and smiled. "We're gonna make sure he knows what a great choice he made." She stood. "I'll be waiting on that call."

"Thanks, Vectra." Will saluted her with his glass before she left the table.

Qasim noticed Minka waving to him the moment he stepped from the elevator into his personal lobby. He acknowledged her wave with a subtle nod and then returned his attention to the man he'd left the elevator with.

"I'll want to see the company's projections for the last five years at least. I also want to know how close they've come to those goals or how far they under or overshot," Qasim said. "I won't have our employees making ill-informed decisions about how to invest *any* of their retirement dollars."

"I agree." Donald Bertson nodded. "You'll have that data before noon tomorrow."

"Don." Qasim smiled, extending his hand for a shake. Don Bertson headed off to the executive offices housed on the other side of the private lobby while Qasim took the opposite route to his office wing and Minka. "Nice to know I've been missed," he said when he reached her.

Minka smiled, but the effort was shaky. "I wanted to catch you before you got caught up in something else."

"Sounds serious." Qasim loosened his tie.

"I don't think so." She shrugged, sending barely a ripple through the shimmering peach fabric of a cap-sleeve blouse. "Probably making something out of nothing anyway."

"Mmm-hmm, it's what I depend on you for, you know?" Qasim inclined his head, slightly arching a heavy brow. "Nothings have a nasty way of turning into somethings."

"Okay." Minka's tone was resolved.

"Hey! Just the two people I wanted to see."

Minka had just rounded her desk when Will Lloyd's greeting rang out.

"Spill it." Qasim settled to a corner of Minka's desk.

"First, let me start off with an apology." He turned to Minka, hand humbly set in the center of his chest. "I'm sorry about how I acted before at the meeting and then again a little while ago for overstepping. I've still got a lot to learn about business

114

etiquette, but I saw a chance and I took it."

"O . . . kay . . ." Frowning curiously, Minka perched on her desk, as well.

"I had drinks with Vectra Bauer this afternoon."

Minka's dark eyes shifted toward Qasim. He'd stilled, his features going sharp.

"Drinks." Qasim felt a muscle stir along his jaw. He didn't care if it showed.

Will didn't appear to notice. "Yeah, we ran into each other after she'd finished up a lunch meeting. We struck up a conversation . . . I see why you like her so much, Sim. She's really nice. Hard to believe she's single."

"Uh, Will." Minka coasted another uneasy look toward Qasim. "You said something about overstepping?"

"Right." He threw back his head slightly in sudden remembrance. "So we got on the subject of her gallery and all her obligations and before I knew it, I'm telling her about what we'd discussed at the meeting about using her place for the scholarship event."

Will fixed Minka with an indulgent look. "I gave you full creds and told Ms. Bauer that the idea had really been yours."

"Did she seem interested?" Minka asked.

"Very." Will took a step closer to the desk. "Even after I told her me and Sim weren't too thrilled about it."

Minka bowed her head to hide a sudden smile.

"She made me see how important it was to do all we could to see that the bulk of the money got in the hands of the folks we're trying to help."

Qasim tugged the loosened tie away from his collar with a touch more force than he actually needed. "Sounds like you talked for quite a while."

"Oh yeah." Will folded his arms over his chest, looking pleased. "She's real easy to talk to. Before I knew it, I was talking about stuff I hadn't thought of in years."

Qasim could feel the stirring jaw muscle positively dancing then. He looped the tie around a half-closed fist and imagined the silken material going around the neck of a man who had once saved his life.

"So, Will, you say she sounds interested in the event?" Minka observed, returning the conversation to more peaceable details.

Will nodded, his honey-toned face reflecting his enthusiasm. "She wants me to call her with a date and time for a dinner meeting. She wants you there and anyone else with a role to play in organizing the event."

Minka quietly sighed, not sure how to respond given the menacing element that had taken hold of Qasim's profile. She opted for diplomacy. "Sounds like a good idea, Will, thanks. I appreciate your diligence."

"Where's this dinner?" Qasim's voice carried a toneless quality. He kept his dark eyes on the tie he had wrapped around his fist.

"Nothing's set. I'm not even sure who all needs to be there." He looked at Minka. "Guess I could use your help deciding how big a deal we want to make this."

"I'll come by your office before quitting time and we'll discuss it," Minka offered. "Thanks for taking the reins on this."

Will smiled broadly. "Just doin' my job." He nodded toward Qasim. "I'll let you get back to work."

Qasim managed to drag himself up out of his agitated haze. "It's good work, Will."

The words seemed to be the encouragement Will was looking for. He knocked a fist conspiratorially against Qasim's upper arm and then set off in the direction of his office.

Minka made a pretense of straightening an already pristine desk. "You're gonna cut off circulation to that hand if you wrap that tie any tighter."

That comment made Qasim smile, and he felt some of his tension wane. "I'm not handling this too well, am I?"

"Well, it *is* Vectra Bauer." Minka shrugged. "Men tend to go stupider than usual over her, I think."

He grunted then eased off the desk. "Amen to that. Keep me posted on this dinner meeting. I want to be there."

"Will do," Minka called.

Heading for his office, Qasim stopped before he rounded the corner. "You wanted to tell me something."

Minka waved a hand. "It can wait."

"No, it can't," he guessed.

She smiled self-consciously. "Something's telling me that my 'nothing' probably really is nothing."

Sim assessed her for an extended moment. "Why the change?"

He'd asked in that way of his that told Minka he wasn't going to let her off the hook without a convincing reason. "Earlier, after the meeting — seeing how . . ." she glanced at the tie still bound around his fist ". . . on edge you were about having the event at Carro's, I decided to take another look at our usual venues."

"And?"

"I wanted to see if there were any we could get to lower their bottom line. I came up with several and planned to run them by you, but then Will came in having worked his magic." She gave a whimsical toss of her bouncy bob. "Talking about it after seemed moot."

"Why do I get the feeling there's more to this?"

Minka's gaze did not falter. She was well aware that her boss had a sixth sense about such things. It was one of the abilities that made him so sensational at his job. The truth was all he would accept, and he'd know if she was giving him less than.

"There's probably more, but at this point I don't think it'll materialize into anything. I stand by what I said. Vectra is our best choice. I honestly don't think she'll charge you a thing to have the event at Carro's."

Qasim winced, the earlier certainty in his expression giving way to a less confident element. "I'm not exactly her favorite person right now."

Minka grinned, her laughter imminent. "Then it's a good thing she doesn't hold a man's stupidity against him."

The dig sent Qasim into a roar of laughter, which carried down the hall as he returned to his office. Alone, Minka's carefree expression tightened. She looked down at a folder, the contents of which she'd very much wanted to share.

CHAPTER 8

Robb DeWitt was happy to open his restaurant for a second private event a week later. That night, Dazzles played host to members of the board for Qasim Wilder's Wilder Warriors Foundation. The fund benefited low-income kids in and around the greater San Francisco area who showed tenacity and perseverance in overcoming obstacles related to school, family and peers that were part of their daily lives.

Each year, Qasim's organization awarded full-ride scholarships to graduating football players from ten area high schools. Qasim greatly disliked the fact that the foundation's board wouldn't allow him to pad the fund with his own money. He would've been just fine with paying for the education of every graduating ball player. Minka, who knew that her boss's generosity bordered on obsession, had given that stipulation.

"Hey!" Vectra gave Minka a tight squeeze.

The woman was first to greet her when she arrived for the dinner meeting.

"Thanks for considering this," Minka whispered.

"No thanks needed." Vectra waved off the gratitude. "I'm happy to do it. Just wish I could've been on the go-to list a lot sooner." She nodded toward one of the Dazzles servers she recognized and then looked back at Minka. "I've attended Sim's charity events every year since they started. I never thought to ask how you guys select the venues." She winced. "Guess I was naive to think the hotels give you a break out of generosity considering the phenomenal work Qasim does right here at home. Low-income kids aren't the only ones who benefit from his attention — there's local government and businesses with national and international notoriety who benefit, too — hotels included."

"Preaching to the choir." Minka gave an exasperated sigh. "Well, they'll miss the business this year. It'll be good to shake things up a bit."

Vectra winked. "Maybe next time around they'll have learned something."

Minka bit her lip, looking a touch uneasy. "Listen, um —" she stepped closer "— Qasim's here."

Vectra blinked and then adopted the same unease as the woman next to her. She looked around, but couldn't make out faces inside Dazzles's dimly lit dining room.

"I heard he wasn't too happy about me being brought in on this."

Minka gave in to a cringe. "It wasn't that, but you guys did have a run-in last week that ended with you looking pretty damn mad when you left the office. He wasn't sure you'd go for it."

"Look, Minka, your boss has a knack for rubbing me the wrong way, but I'm above letting that stop me from helping out for a good cause."

"And that's what I told him."

Vectra shifted her weight from one mauve pump to the other. "Was he concerned about that?"

"He's protective of you, Vectra. Anybody can see that."

Vectra knew that very well and silently noted that Qasim was so protective that he'd included himself among the list of things she needed to be shielded from.

"Well, the gang's all here, and Robb DeWitt's turning down business so he can accommodate us," Vectra noted.

Minka glanced toward the dining room. "We believe he'll think it's worth it."

"Well, Will made a very convincing argument when we talked, but it wouldn't have taken much to get my support."

Minka leaned close again, this time making a pretense of acting secretive. "Don't tell him that. He's feeling pretty proud of himself for reeling you in."

Vectra threw back her head, laughing. Then, she and Minka headed into the softly lit, conversation-studded dining room.

The dinner meeting with the Wilder Warriors Foundation board and members of the Wilder Corporation turned into more of a dinner celebration almost within a half hour of it getting started. Vectra listened avidly to the proposal put together by Will Lloyd's team. She then presented the group with the news that she not only loved the idea of holding the soiree at Carro but that she'd love it even more if they accepted her offer of sponsoring the event free of charge. While everyone was thrilled by the offer, there were those who wanted to make certain their generous benefactor understood what she was saying no to.

"Ms. Bauer, we're all over the moon right now, but this *is* a weekend event — it's why we tend to use hotels as the venue," Xander Battle, a foundation board member noted.

"The hotels did throw us for a loop this year with their price quotes, but we understand that such a gathering isn't . . . inexpensive."

"I'm aware of that." Vectra smiled, taking no offense. "My home is very well equipped. The main house and the vineyard have been photographed on numerous occasions and for well-known national and international publications. We're equipped with two kitchens — one residential, the other industrial — both more than adequate to handle all meals and individual dining requests. The last isn't my opinion, but the opinion of your selected caterer and the esteemed proprietor of Dazzles." She waved toward Robb DeWitt, who had joined in for the meeting.

"And I wholeheartedly agree," Robb admitted amidst laughter from the group.

Qasim was the only one, in fact, who didn't share in the laughter. He was seated almost directly across from Vectra at the wide round table, which was candlelit and beautifully set for the evening's dinner.

"Ms. Bauer," Qasim called, drawing everyone's attention and silence, "I think what Xander's referring to is the money you're turning your back on by offering us the use of your home at no charge."

"Qasim's right, Ms. Bauer," Jennifer

French, seated nearest to her board colleague Xander Battle, agreed. "It's an awful lot of money. Even when the hotels are at their most reasonable, they rake in quite a hefty sum of cash for our events."

Vectra's lovely face was further softened by the indulgent smile gracing her mouth. "I appreciate you guys for looking out for me, but I honestly want no payment for this. Carro isn't hurting for cash — especially none that pulls funds away from a worthy cause like this."

"Hear, hear!" someone cheered, and many raised their glasses in toast.

"Besides," Vectra called, "I'm looking forward to all the fun we'll have. I rarely have anyone out for sleepovers."

The group burst into laughter. Everyone's concerns seemed to have abated. Sadly, Qasim was still not in the mood for humor. The fact was never more evident than when he watched Will Lloyd, seated right next to Vectra, lean over to whisper into her ear.

Vectra laughed, whispering something back to Will, followed by the clinking of their water glasses together. Qasim finished what remained of his bourbon and motioned to one of the waitstaff for another. Never had he regretted his high tolerance for alcohol more than in that moment.

■ ■ ■ ■

Vectra hadn't been oblivious to the evident disapproval radiating from Qasim's side of the table. It would've been difficult to miss, given the blaring intensity of the glare he fixed her way. She didn't know why the hell he was so upset with her.

Though she'd been happy to do it, she had, after all, given his foundation quite a magnanimous gift by agreeing to accommodate a tremendous event at no charge. The guy could at least show a *little* gratitude. Yet he preferred to sit in his chair like a king on high and glower at her.

Thankfully, Will Lloyd's good nature had taken the edge off. His wickedly amusing comments had kept her laughing. She hadn't taken any of what he said seriously. Aside from his first comment, which had been in response to her sleepover tease, the rest of his remarks had been overheard and enjoyed by everyone on their end of the outrageously huge round table.

The meeting was drawing to a close. The board had trickled out first, followed by most of the Wilder executive staff. Only Minka and Will remained along with Qasim and Vectra. Robb DeWitt had gone to handle closing procedures with his staff. Minka was the first of the foursome to say her good-nights. And then, there were three.

Qasim's sour mood went from bad to worse. He'd almost forgotten how talkative his old friend could be — especially when the topic opened up to old army stories. Will's favorite: how he'd saved Sim's life.

The retelling of his least flattering moment was a story Qasim could've done without. Still, he was willing to sit through it for the opportunity to study Vectra's reaction. He watched the expressions change on her lovely face and was intrigued by the horror and honest concern he witnessed as she listened to detail after detail of the events leading up to his traumatic ordeal.

A woman's love and affection can be the best kind of therapy, Robb DeWitt had said.

Qasim realized how very much he wanted to experience what they meant firsthand. Furthermore, he wanted to experience them with Vectra Bauer, regardless of what all his damned voices of reason told him.

He wanted her, and she'd made it more than clear that she wanted him. He'd never been one to deny going after what he really wanted. The reasons he'd denied himself seemed flimsy. Maybe once he'd given in to

127

his curiosity about what she was like in bed, he could move on. He didn't buy that for a second, but it sounded good.

Qasim tuned back into his table partners. Will had evidently wrapped up his war story and was working on snagging an invite back to Vectra's.

Vectra was silently warning herself not to look across the table at Qasim. It wouldn't be a pretty sight, she knew, given the fact that he'd already threatened one of their best friends with bodily harm for simply wanting to pick up a phone to call her. Having his employee, old army buddy or not, offer to take her home had to be weighing heavy on the flimsiest tether of his restraint.

She stood. "Thanks for the offer, Will. Um —" she eased her tote strap across her shoulder "— I've got my car."

She had to admit she was rather taken aback by the offer. For most of the night, Will Lloyd had been friendly and engaging. Now, she all too easily recognized the more suggestive tinge to his manner. Obviously, she'd been more fixed on Qasim than she thought. She'd completely misread what Will was putting out.

"I don't mind driving your car," Will flirted outlandishly, standing too and nudging Vectra's shoulder with his own. "I could take a cab from your place in the morning."

Vectra looked to Qasim, noting that some new demonic element had rippled to life in his dark stare.

"Um, Will —" she patted his arm "— maybe another time." She paused, observing that her unintentional promise had brought Qasim to his feet. She swallowed hard. "Good night." Quietly, she left the table having no desire to linger and witness the upcoming carnage of Will Lloyd's soon-to-be-broken body strewn about the Dazzles dining room.

Will followed Vectra's departure, his attractive features alight with approval. "Damn, she's something else. I wouldn't mind —" He gave a start, turning to find Qasim right next to him.

"Sim, man, what —"

"Stay away from her."

Will gaped. "Sim?"

"You don't talk to her." Qasim breathed the words with stony intensity while stoically observing the man. "I get that it's damn near impossible not to look at her, but you'd do well to remember to make those glances brief if I'm anywhere around. Am I understood?"

Stunned, Will could only manage a few rapid nods. Robb returned to the dining room, and Qasim went to say his goodnights. Alone, Will settled his weight to the edge of the round table where he fought to slow his breathing.

Vectra returned home in time to take one of the housekeepers up on an offer for a pot of tea. She was still a little too unsteady for sleep after having practically sped home, and appreciated the offer. While her tea was being prepared, she headed up to change into more suitable lounge attire. She returned downstairs to see off the housekeeper for the evening. She then indulged in the steamy pot of jasmine tea the woman had been so kind to set out in the library.

The night had turned cool, and the tea satisfied dual needs for warmth and nerve-soothing. Of course, Vectra realized the nerve-soothing would probably require a little more work. She considered spiking the tea with a touch of coconut rum.

She'd known Qasim well over two years. Until that night, she would have bet good money on the fact that he was one of the most even-tempered men she knew. Most often, that had to be the face he normally wore, but earlier that evening, she'd glimpsed the dangerous man he told her lurked inside.

Sure, he'd *told* her, but she hadn't listened. She certainly hadn't fully believed it, despite the instincts that advised her not to underestimate him. What she'd witnessed in the bottomless depths of his stare had been sheer rage directed at a man who'd had the nerve to proposition her. She certainly didn't envy being in the spot Will Lloyd had perhaps unknowingly put himself in. Still, witnessing Qasim's reactions that night was quite an eye-opener. An intriguing one that drew her in, like a moth to flame.

Vectra finished off her mug of tea and moved to pour another from the stout pot sitting on the tray. She was grateful that her hands weren't shaking quite as much. She had scarcely sipped the second cup when the knock hit the front door.

She stood, indulging in another hasty sip before rushing out to the foyer. She stopped abruptly, exercising caution before she welcomed the unexpected visitor.

"Who is it?"

"Open the door."

The order, gruffly given in a voice she recognized, galvanized her into movement.

Disengaging the locks, she slowly pulled the door open until Qasim filled the entrance and forced the door wide to grant himself admittance. Vectra backed up, the sounds of her house shoes echoing against the foyer's blush-tinted marble flooring.

"Qasim —"

"Where's your staff?"

"Gone. I —"

The additional words caught and disintegrated in her throat when Qasim's hands folded over her hips and he crushed her to the wall of muscle that was his chest. His mouth slammed hard upon hers, and Vectra granted him instant access. Her tongue was at first too stunned to reciprocate the savagely sensual treatment it received from his.

Qasim was unable to stifle his soft moans while his tongue swept the even ridge of her back teeth. Then, he once again tangled his tongue with hers.

There was a break in the kiss. Vectra studied him in disbelief as she swallowed and attempted to steady her breathing. "I thought you said —"

"Forget what I said." He crushed her mouth beneath his again, drawing her close and swinging her slight form up high against his. One forearm was at her back while the other provided a steely shelf for her bent knees.

Vectra rounded up whatever lingering questions she may've had and tossed them as far and deep into the recesses of her mind as she could manage. The questions still mattered, but they took a definite backseat to the fact that Qasim Wilder had at last cast aside the issues that had resulted in keeping them from enjoying what they'd both wanted for some time.

She arched closer, hungering to seal any space separating them. Greedily, her nails threaded through the hair cut close at his nape. The fine, silken strands sparked delightful tingles along her fingertips and beckoned her even closer.

She didn't care what he tasted in her kiss. She was too desperate — too sex-starved? Perhaps. In that moment, she'd proudly admit it. She'd sealed herself away from the most enjoyable aspects of living for too long. She just hadn't wanted to deal with the possible headaches. In truth, she'd found no reason that made it worth the true effort to do so.

The physical manifestation of Qasim Wilder was reason enough, and she damn well intended to enjoy every moment.

Qasim had maintained his stance in the

foyer, simply treasuring the reality of Vectra in his arms. The past few days that had passed since the party had been literal hell. Kissing her had been a mistake. The fact that he'd done it hadn't been the mistake. Rather, it was the fact that he'd not done everything in his power to see that it had followed through to its logical and very much desired conclusion.

He'd left her house the other night agitated mentally, sexually and every way in between. Sitting across from her at that meeting tonight it was all he could do not to snatch her up and take what he'd imagined. He'd dreamed of her so incessantly that his sleep lately had been a joke.

Vectra's faint moan as she lunged and twirled her tongue about his had drained all strength from his legs. His eyelids even felt weighted down by the power of his reaction to her, and he gave thanks then for his eidetic memory.

The almost supernatural ability for vivid imagery recall would suit him well that night. Vectra's innocently hospitable offer to show him around the upper levels of her home had secured a blueprint of the area in his mind. He retraced each detail of every square foot of the house until he located the room he sought.

Vectra's bedroom suite was a luscious balance of opulence tempered by simplicity. Golden illumination poured down softly from the recessed lighting and end-table lamps that burned low from various points throughout the sumptuous space. The color scheme of the room was a soothing mixture of gold, coral, plum and rich maple. A gold comforter lay on the king-size bed, which was supported by a maple bed frame. Wide, unlit candles held a stately presence from their perches inside tall, sculpted holders finished in gleaming brass. Once inside her room, Qasim turned with Vectra still in his arms and kissed her soundly. Then he used the hand under her knees to lock the door.

Vectra fisted a heap of his shirt when he suddenly withdrew from their kiss. Expectantly, she searched the smoldering obsidian of his gaze, swearing to herself that she would do him serious bodily harm if he told her they couldn't do this.

"What?" Her tone was impatience at its height.

"Tonight. What'd Will say to you?"

Some of her anxiety eased when she noted the devilish glint in his stare. She knew exactly what he was referring to and smiled.

"He said it was a shame I hadn't had a sleepover in so long."

Something humorous merged with the predatory shadows in his stare, and Vectra's heart surged with anticipation and sweltering arousal.

Qasim grinned. "He was right."

Chapter 9

The only thing better than kissing Vectra Bauer had to be leaving her mouth free to release the most sensually tortured, ego-boosting gasps.

Her cotton jumper was pleasingly accessible, but he wanted it gone. Need coursed like a fever over the desire to have her naked under him. He didn't want to unsettle her or rush the chance to study the parts of her he'd only been able to imagine bare.

Her breasts were beautiful — naturally firm and full caramel-toned mounds that held him rapt with fascination when they heaved with her breaths. He loved the way one molded to his palm, almost, but not quite, filling it.

His thumb crested the chocolate nub that protruded from the brown sugar–toned disc surrounding it. The move forced another ribbon of the ego-stroking sounds, and Qasim rested his face in the crook of her softly fragrant neck. He wanted to savor the hitched cries he caused.

Vectra bit her lip not to stifle sounds of pleasure, but to prevent herself from begging him to do more. Not that what he was doing wasn't heavenly, erotic and sensational. If he continued, though, she wasn't going to last, and she so very much wanted to orgasm with him inside her.

Qasim seemed just fine right where he was. Still fully clothed, he kept one of her bare thighs flat beneath his trouser-clad one.

The position left Vectra free of most of his crushing weight, but she wanted more. She wanted it all. She whimpered again as her hips began a slow rhythm of anticipation upon the bed.

Qasim moved, as well. The hand cupping her breast skimmed its underside then journeyed beyond her ribs, across her stomach and down to the waxed triangle of skin above her core. When he simultaneously sucked a nipple and pressed a long, thick finger into her sex, her whimpering mounted into open-mouthed sobs of ecstasy with every movement of his hand. In moments, she was in the throes of her first climax.

Qasim raised his head to watch her react to his touch. Possessiveness locked in, full and viselike, inside the most basic part of him. Qasim knew in that moment that she was never getting rid of him. The sounds she uttered and the captivating artistry of her were only for him.

She was for him.

Qasim mentally shook off the idea. He didn't want to focus on matters he hadn't quite worked out with the moment at hand. Her luminous eyes opened and settled on his face. He could feel her intimately fisting around his finger, milking all remnants of sensation even as she came down just a fraction from her peak.

He saw apology in her gaze amidst her satisfaction. There was regret that she'd so suddenly lost control.

"I want to see that again," he told her before she could do anything foolish like apologize for coming without him.

"Sim," she said. She'd uttered his nickname.

It was something she'd never done in all the time he'd known her. He had planned to take his time with her, had practically broken every traffic law en route to driving there that night thinking about the ways he'd intended to do that.

There would be time, he swore even as he willed restraint to assert itself. Pointless. He was too far gone with desire that had taken root long ago.

Vectra felt her heart thud at an almost deafening intensity when he started to remove his clothes. He'd worn a simple, yet finely crafted milk-chocolate crew shirt beneath a sports jacket of a darker chocolate. The colors were gorgeous against his perfect licorice skin. She could hear herself swallow as he peeled off the jacket to reveal stunningly corded forearms. The muscular planks flexed and captured her attention as he reached into the inner pocket of his jacket and drew a nice supply of condoms.

Vectra's lashes fluttered, anticipation taking flight once more as the sound of cascading packets hit a far-off section of the big bed. She didn't look in the direction they settled. She was too riveted by Qasim doffing his shirt.

One tug to the collar at the back of his neck eased the garment up his back and over his head. Vectra gasped when she saw his chest. She'd known he was built, but even their recent closeness hadn't come close to preparing her for the sight of him with no barriers. He seemed more massive than his expensive suits implied.

His pecs were heavy slabs of dark, packed

muscle above his carved abs. Vectra reached out, needing to prove that he was really there and hers for the touching.

Qasim captured her hand, resting it flat against one granite pec and pulling her from her back in a fluid move. Vectra found herself straddling his lap, and she shivered when her nipples nudged and caressed his. Kissing resumed again, and with it, the ravenous sounds of unsated lust. Vectra took her fill of his X-rated torso, nails raking every inch of skin she touched.

Qasim tunneled his fingers into her short, dark hair, cradling her head as he caged her beneath him again. He took infinite care, evidently fearing he'd smother her with his bulk. He kept one hand fisted near her ribs on the bed, bracing a forearm to support his weight. She tugged, wrapping her long legs about his waist and moaning amidst the kiss. She loved the way he felt covering her.

Qasim cradled Vectra's head. All the while, he drove his tongue deeply into her mouth, which he also filled with his guttural groans.

Vectra felt an insistent pressure against her inner thigh, and she laughed appreciatively when she realized Qasim was undoing his belt and trouser fastening. She assisted, smoothing her hands over massive

141

shoulders and across the sinewy plane of his back. Her fingers skimmed just below the waistband of his trousers and boxers.

Her plans to help slide them away became sidetracked by his toned ass. She hungrily squeezed while easing him nearer to her aching femininity.

None-too-gentle sounds funneled up from Qasim's chest as any and all patience fled. He broke their kiss, panting out labored moans as his head rested on her clavicle, and he jerked out of what was left of his clothing.

Vectra was certain she hadn't reached her limit of adoration upon his incredible body. She was right. Once freed, his erection jutted magnificently, and she reflexively licked her lips as questions surged. The most prevalent of which was, *Is it as good as it looks?*

Dazedly, she cupped him in a loose fist, testing the length and weight of him. Closing her hand around him was impossible. Orgasmic sensations stirred at what weighted her palm. Anticipation had her swooning while her imagination ran wild conjuring what he'd feel like inside her.

Qasim rocked his hips into the cradle of her palm. Teeth bared, he lightly grazed them across her collarbone as the mock thrusts gained pace.

Vectra was awed by his reaction, her own ego stroked by the power she experienced over the devastating male in her bed. Motivated by his helpless responses, she emboldened her touch, swiping her thumb across the slit at the flawless mushroom crown of his shaft. Faint traces of his need glistened there.

The move had an overwhelming effect on Qasim. He suddenly snatched at her hand. Another few moments and he'd have spent himself in her palm.

Vectra watched him go still, securing her wrist as he worked to steady himself.

We can't have that, she thought.

She used her free hand to feel across the bed until it connected with one of the foil condom wrappers.

The slight crinkle of the packaging caught Qasim's ear, and he lifted his head toward the sound. Expression unreadable, he sat up over her and waited. Silently, he gave her reign to apply their protection. He held himself still, but looked ready to melt when she gloved his erection in her satiny hold and tortured him with a few slow, agonizing pumps.

"Vectra . . . please . . ."

She smiled. He was so very much the way

she would have him, she decided, but refused to get sidetracked by the fact. She hadn't meant to tease him, but the man was walking enticement. An enticement that was, at the moment, naked in her bed. She was entitled to more than a little groping.

Qasim had more than groping in mind once the condom was stretched over his engorged arousal. He took no heed of the gasp she uttered when his hands covered her knees and dragged her to the middle of the tangled bed. He held her thighs open to accept his wide frame, and his mind was trained on a singular command.

Take.

A broken sob coasted from Vectra's throat when she felt the delicious intrusion of his body inside hers. Still, her intimate walls protested. They'd not been used . . . properly . . . in quite some time. Qasim, merciless in the lust haze clouding his brain, pressed forward, coaxing her sex to yield to his. He exhaled on a curse when her muscles stretched to accommodate the broad head of his erection and the broader length that followed.

He took no notice of whether he was crushing her, and Vectra was glad.

"Sim." She gave herself over to whatever he would have of her.

Once she'd taken the crown of his sex and a few more inches, he eased the rest home in a swift drive until he was fully seated and marking her with the depth of his strokes.

Qasim wanted to watch every moment of her taking him but could feel his lids growing heavy as desire heightened, weakening and strengthening him at once. He held her thighs wider apart, keeping them trapped on the bed as he hunched over her. He cupped a heaving breast, holding it still for sensual attention from his generous mouth. All the while, his lean hips rocked, pumping her with an intensity that incited ragged cries until Vectra had grown hoarse.

She slid her hands from her hair and fisted them against his biceps. Climactic spasms racked her body in tandem with Qasim's. She was sensitive enough to feel him flooding the condom with his seed, and the pleasure of that sensation overloaded her senses and she peaked once more.

He suckled her breast in earnest then. He was thoroughly spent but still reeled from the amazing aftershocks of her sugar walls squeezing and releasing his sex of every ounce of his need.

Vectra's heart reclaimed its thudding intensity when the sound of another crinkling foil packet reached her ears.

■ ■ ■ ■

"Sim?" Vectra lifted her face from the pillow and then let her head fall back into to the cushiony cradle as a new wave of exhaustion claimed her.

"Vectra?"

"Mmm . . . ? Sim . . ." Her face was partially hidden by the pillow, muffling her voice.

"Vectra?"

There was knocking, followed by a voice that was definitely not Qasim's.

"Charlotte?" Vectra murmured, awareness beginning its slow intrusion upon her sleep-addled brain.

She rolled to her back, wincing. Stabs of discomfort, swaddled in a pleasant ache, sent her intimate muscles throbbing and clenching for something that was no longer there. Qasim had evidently taken his leave.

Vectra didn't want to spend too much time on how she felt about that. Gingerly, she slid toward the edge of the bed, vaguely wondering where her comforter was. She found it, her toes sinking into the thick, satiny covering after she swung her legs down from the bed. She picked it up, wrapped herself in it and began an awkward shuffle toward the bedroom door. Sensual bruising caused her to throb more insistently, and Vectra silently chanted, *Careful what you wish for.*

Charlotte Sweeney looked decidedly ruffled when Vectra found her on the other side of the door. Vectra read the worry and curiosity in the small woman's cinnamon-brown gaze.

Vectra raised a weary hand. "Sorry about the locked door, Char. I was exhausted last night, made worse by a boring business dinner in the city." She explained, figuring Qasim must have set the lock on her bedroom door handle before he left.

"Wendy made a cup of that knockout tea when I got here and I was ready for bed in minutes." Silently, Vectra acknowledged that while it wasn't the absolute truth it wasn't an *entire* falsehood.

Charlotte bought it. The concern in her gaze gave way to sympathy. "Poor thing," she crooned, already reaching for the bedroom door handle. "Well, I'm glad to see you're finally giving in to the rest you obviously need. Beautiful girls shouldn't burn the candle at both ends — puts bags under the eyes." She reached up to lovingly pinch Vectra's cheek. "Back to bed with you," she ordered.

"Oh, Char no, I've got meetings in the gallery all day —"

Charlotte raised a firm hand. "They can wait. I'm requiring two more hours of sleep — at least."

"Charlotte . . ." Vectra whined, believing she should at least protest a little longer.

"Do you need me to come in there and put you into bed?" Charlotte propped fists to her round hips.

"All right, all right." Vectra remembered all the condom wrappers she and Qasim had worked through the night before, and she wasn't eager to explain the mess Charlotte was sure to find if she took another step inside the room.

"Lovely." Pleased by Vectra's obliging attitude, Charlotte took a step back from the door. "I'll be back later with breakfast." She blew Vectra a kiss and then shut the door behind her.

Vectra sighed, admitting that a couple more hours of sleep did sound quite heavenly. She turned, shuffling back toward the bed while taking a quick survey of the elaborately designed rug covering the hardwood floor.

Perhaps Qasim did take the time to spruce up before he made his quiet exit, she thought.

She found no evidence of their vivacious

romps from the night before. There were tangled covers barely clinging to the mattress and throw pillows that had either been kicked to the floor or hurtled to the other side of the room. Otherwise, the place was decidedly tidy. Still, she wished he'd told her goodbye. She bristled, flopping to the bed and punching the comforter when the billowing gold material poofed out about her.

Stop it.

He left the way anyone would after a one-night stand.

That's what it was, wasn't it?

That *is* what she alluded to him, that she was okay with it, right? He'd given her what she'd wanted . . . *Boy, had he ever* . . . She couldn't fault him for treating it for what it was the next morning.

In the distance, she picked up the ring of an old-fashioned rotary phone — her mobile. The device was still tucked away in her purse, which she'd tossed to the chaise near the closet room when she'd come up to change the night before.

Vectra debated, really wanting her sleep and knowing it could be work calling. Cursing at her weakness, she pushed off the bed and went to track down the phone.

Qasim's name was on the display.

149

Her heart slammed against her ribs.

She dropped into the lounge chair, and the comforter poofed around her again.

"Qasim." She swallowed an attempt to urge her leaping heart to return to its rightful position.

"Hey."

Vectra melted and wasn't ashamed of the reaction. His voice was as thick and rich as a chocolate cascade — and just as tempting.

"Are you okay?"

A throb began to stir. Hell, if his voice wasn't an aphrodisiac of the most sinful variety.

"I, um . . . I thought I was okay, and then I woke up and you weren't here." There. She'd said it. God could she be more pathetic?

"I didn't think you'd want to explain to your staff why I was there."

She laughed. "Are you serious? They'd have probably thrown us a party. They think I'm alone in this house too much."

"Can I see you?"

"When?" She groaned.

Pathetic.

Evidently, a night of amazing and exhausting sex hadn't gotten the man out of her system. She heard him chuckling. The sound rolled softly through the phone line, sinful indeed.

"Today?" he suggested. "That'd mean driving back into the city."

"Not a problem. I've got gallery meetings to get back for."

"Will anyone miss you if you spend the night with me?"

The question caused her core muscles to constrict on the stimulation it alone provided.

Breathe, Vectra . . .

"I'll leave a note for the staff telling them I decided to stay over with Dad. I do that a lot and they wouldn't feel the need to check. They'd only call my cell if they do."

"What time can I see you?"

Vectra bit her lip before responding with an eager *"Anytime."* She already felt pathetic enough with her verbal responses thus far. No need to push the envelope toward anxious. She'd probably done that already, though. She lay back on the chaise, squeezing her thighs in an effort to quell the needy stabs targeting her sex.

"The gallery closes at eight-thirty," she told him. "We're prepping for a show, and the artist and her people have arranged to be out by then during the week."

"I'll pick you up at nine, then."

"Qasim, you don't have —"

"I'll see you at nine, Vec." It wasn't a question.

"Okay." She waited until the connection ended on his line. Then, she moaned a little in reaction to the mini-spasms that rocked her center and demanded to be satisfied. She resisted the urge to tend to the ache herself. Only Qasim was qualified to do that effectively.

The end of her day couldn't get there fast enough.

CHAPTER 10

Qasim considered calling Vectra again the second he ended the call. He wanted out of his office and back inside the master bedroom suite at Carro Vineyard.

Easy, Sim.

He grunted a harsh laugh. "Right," he muttered, his voice creeping up on a growl.

Sex with Vectra had been like dousing thirst from a canteen after a year in the desert. There was no such thing as enough, and, man, hadn't he proven that. He'd been way too rough with her, he feared, recalling how delicate her lithe, curvy frame felt in his hands.

Once he had her in his arms, his better intentions had been wiped from his consciousness. *Taking* had been the only intention worth seeing to. Stamina set his body on continuous refuel, and he'd only stopped because she'd been exhausted.

He would take more care with her tonight,

he swore. He had a feeling that he'd not let her out of his bed when morning came. He'd take his time, give her more foreplay. Heaven knew he wanted to do that last night, but she'd tapped into every hormone he possessed, driving them into a state of sheer lust that was only soothed when he had his hands or mouth somewhere on her body.

Her smell, a unique mix of melon and perhaps lavender, took that lust haze of his into overdrive. He'd always imagined what she'd taste like and had planned to make her climax with his mouth as he had with his fingers. He'd been aching to know how she'd taste as her moisture coated his tongue while he took her with it.

He hissed out a ragged curse. Leaning forward in his desk chair, he massaged his eyes with the heels of his palms. The office was definitely not the place to fantasize. Qasim reached for one of the remotes in the desk caddy. He'd prefer reaching for something else, but the office was *most* definitely not the place to . . . handle what fantasizing had done to his body.

He raised the volume on one of the overhead plasma screens and allowed the ramblings of the sports commentators to redirect his thoughts. The morning show did the trick, and he was feeling more like himself by the time a knock hit the door. Qasim admitted his first visitor of the day.

Will stuck his head just inside the office. "Hey, man," he said in a slow, measured style as though he was trying to get a bead on his mood.

"What's goin' on, Will?" Qasim's friendly comeback was genuine. Despite their earlier tension regarding Vectra, a talk with Will would certainly keep his thoughts on safer ground.

If Will had been wearing a hat, it would've been in his hand. He stepped inside the office, closing the door with more care than was probably needed. When he finally turned, one hand rested in the center of his chest a deliberate display of humbleness.

"Sim, man —" he shook his head, appearing stunned in his disbelief "— my apologies. Attribute my stupidity last night to one too many drinks and a foot that wouldn't stay out of my mouth. I had no idea it was like that between you and Ms. Bauer." He swallowed, risking a step closer to the multisectional desk area. "I didn't know she was yours."

Qasim responded with an anguished smile. "She's not mine." He dismissed the way his heart twisted inside his chest. It was

155

a sensation he only experienced when he lied. "I never should've come off that way," he said.

"You've known her for a long time, right?"

"That's right."

Will seemed to be gnawing the inside of his cheek. "Excuse me for pointing out the fact that she's an obvious dime." He slightly raised a hand in caution.

"Excused." A corner of Qasim's mouth tilted to a smile.

"Man," Will exhaled the word on an amused sigh, "are you really okay with a 'just friends' relationship or did you wind up there by mistake?"

Qasim burst into laughter despite how deeply his old friend had rattled his nerves the night before. "I very much want to change my 'just friends' status with her," he admitted because it felt so damn good to say it to someone.

Will moved another step closer to the desk. "So what's stopping you?"

"The fact that I'm an idiot probably has a lot to do with it."

Will took his turn at bursting into laughter before he sobered. "You know, Sim, unless you plan on threatening to break in half every guy who acts interested in the lovely Ms. Bauer, you'd do well to stake your claim. Women like that don't remain unattached for long."

"I understand and agree." Qasim commenced rubbing his eyes again.

"Apologies for the nosiness, man." Will gave another cautious wave. "I only wanted to come by and explain myself. I can't afford to lose another job over something stupid coming out of my mouth." He shrugged. "Guess I just need to think twice before I stop attending my AA meetings, after all."

"We're good, man. Your job is safe."

"I appreciate it, Sim." Will's nod was reverent. "I'll catch you later, man. Hey, you want to grab dinner after work?" he asked.

"Plans tonight, but catch me another time?"

"Count on it." Will gave an airy salute and left the office soon after.

Qasim tried to focus on one of the folders containing items that needed his reply and signature by day's end. He had been working for ten minutes when he recalled that he hadn't seen Will drink a thing the night before.

"You know you're free to get more outrageous with the décor, Yancey. We've had artists take our 'design your own theme' offers to some pretty wild places."

Yancey Croachman laughed. "I can imagine!" Her pale blue eyes sparkled as she looked around the bright, spacious elegance of Gallery V. After a few moments, however, her smile waned.

"There was a time I would've been the wildest of the bunch. Just ask Cooper," Yancey said, referring to her agent. "My mood now has definitely mellowed." She clasped her hands to a surprisingly ample chest for someone her size. "The work in this latest collection needs a mellow environment in order to sing. The hidden jewels nestled inside all the overt busyness of the pieces pop even more when uncovered while the observer is enveloped in a peaceful oasis."

Vectra, her cheek propped against her fist, began to shake her head dazedly. "Wow . . . you're sure to leave this showing a millionaire with a sales pitch like that. I can't imagine a buyer not wanting to have one of these pieces on a wall in their favorite room."

Yancey's expression, while serene, glinted with an element that made her seem far older. "I came from a place that was all too real for me. It's taken me a long time to get here."

Vectra's brow furrowed just slightly. She felt somewhat eclipsed by the solemn manner that wafted about the young artist. "You sound like you've got quite a story to tell," she noted.

Yancey shrugged. "It was one I was glad to see end." She closed her eyes briefly. "I was in an abusive relationship — high school sweethearts, hmph. Started our junior year in high school, lasted through college. Our mothers were friends. I knew him since playpens and diapers."

"Yancey, I —" Vectra felt her stomach muscles clenching. "I'm sorry."

Yancey's smile was surprisingly serene. "When I was finally able to draw myself out of the wicked spell I was under and see that it was *my* life I was jeopardizing, I was able to stop being ruled by everybody else's image of us. We were the adorable childhood sweethearts destined to be adult soul mates. Anyway . . . that's when the rest of my life began."

Yancey sighed approvingly and turned back to the canvas she and Vectra stood closest to. She gave a wave. "That's where all this comes from."

"Would you do it again, Yancey?" Vectra

didn't mean to voice the question aloud. She wanted — needed — to hear the other woman's answer. "Would you get serious?" she asked. "Really serious about another man? Could you? After something like that?"

Yancey folded her arms over her chest, hiding a portion of the Canadian flag emblazoned across the T-shirt she sported with faded jeans. She rocked to and fro, appearing to contemplate her answer.

"I've believed for a long time now that living, *wanting* to live, is the best therapy." Light returned, full-blown, into her bright gaze. "I hope there will be another chance to do it again, because I plan to give it my all and do it better than it's ever been done before."

She shared a saucy wink. "So long as he's worth it, and I have a feeling that I'll know if he is. Maybe . . . through the chaos of my past, he'll be waiting in the mellow depths of a possible future." Yancey waved toward the canvas again.

Vectra parroted the move. "You've just made your first sale. Let's go up to my office so I can cut you a check."

"Quittin' time?" Will called out to Minka as he approached her desk.

Minka grinned. "Just about. If you're looking for Qasim, he's still in his office."

"We already talked earlier today." Will presented a folder. "I only came by the drop off these copies for the foundation files."

"Thanks," Minka drawled, satisfied as she accepted the folder secured by a large binder clip.

Will was looking toward the corridor beyond the sun-drenched lobby that led to the president's office. "So . . . Sim and Vectra Bauer, huh? I didn't know 'til today how caught up he was over her. Did you see that coming?"

"Saw it coming a long time ago."

Will whistled, impressed. "On that note," he tipped an imaginary cap, "have a good night, Ms. Gerald."

Minka reciprocated in kind, and once Will had gone, she debated on whether to crack into the folder before heading home for the day.

"Ahh . . . what the hell . . ." she decided to get the lingering work out of the way in order to start her morning with a clear desk. Besides, the folder may not have been as formidable as it looked.

To Minka's delight, the file mostly consisted of invoices. She made note of every sort of paper document that went into

161

the president's library. Invoices were the easiest to note for her electronic records. Other items required not only a document name, but also a brief overview of its contents.

Minka kicked off her pumps and settled in behind her computer. She'd cleared a quarter of the invoices when she came to a stack from Dazzles. She smiled, recalling the dinner meeting the night before. It had been work that felt like a party, and she'd had a great time.

The reminiscent smile lost some of its illumination, though, when she shuffled the invoices. Her brows drew close, faintly marring the delicate skin between them. Maybe she did need to head home because what she was looking at made no sense.

She was stunned, but not relatively so by the spike in the hotel price quotes. The economy had sent so much off kilter. But this? She stood, moving to another section of her gargantuan desk.

The purposely uncluttered area allowed Minka to spread out material for detailed projects. She used the space to spread out all the invoices and review them for pricing and services rendered. Taking her diligence a step further, she pulled invoices specific to Dazzles for the previous year's event.

"What the hell . . . ?" she breathed.

Vectra was still padding around barefoot in her office by the time the gallery closed for the evening. The Croachman team had left around 8:15 p.m. Yancey was riding another high cloud because of the unexpected sale she made that afternoon thanks to Vectra. The young artist and her team were eager to head out for a bit of celebrating.

Vectra left her staff to handle the closing of the gallery while she returned to her office. The day had been a productive one. She'd even had the chance to settle on a date for a tasting with the Dazzles chef staff in preparation for the Wilder Warriors Foundation event.

She wondered if anyone noticed how excited she was over the event — over *any* event that involved Qasim. Vectra wouldn't admit she was favoring his gatherings over any others she might be involved with. Yet she couldn't deny that it did crazy things to her heart to know she could be a help to the man she was falling in love with.

In love? Where did *that* revelation come from?

Can it, Vectra.

It hadn't come out of nowhere. It was, after all, why she'd been so upset by his sudden retreat from their friendship, right?

She shook her head, raking her nails through the elegant, clipped locks of her pixie style. She needed to back off that train of thought. She didn't even know the man, for goodness' sake! They had been friends in the truest sense of the word. Nothing romantic had reared its head before.

But that wasn't true, was it?

Qasim had admitted to backing away and that wanting her had a lot to do with it. She'd already confessed that her attraction had gone beyond the platonic level.

Attraction and want — that had been the extent of it. No one had said a thing about love.

"And no one's about to start." With a wave, she filed the decision to a far corner of her mind and fixed her attention on her latest acquisition.

She had Yancey's painting brought up to her office. She didn't want to risk it being left down on the floor and seen by another perspective buyer. The fact that it had already been sold might not matter. Vectra had seen people become totally resistant to viewing other work once one piece sparked that desire. The fact that the piece belonged to another and that the *other* was the gallery's owner could easily put Vectra in the uncomfortable position of having to sell it. Either that or risk losing a future patron.

Better safe than sorry, she reasoned and went to collect the canvas. She'd been toying with the idea of hanging the piece in her office and considered a wall behind the gray sectional sofa that hugged it. Canvas in hand, she stepped up onto the sofa and positioned the piece on the wall as she judged the location.

It took only a few minutes for Vectra to decide she'd prefer to enjoy Yancey Croachman's captivating work from the privacy of her own home. Carefully, she eased the canvas to the floor, leaning it along one of the sofa arms.

"Nice."

Vectra had just straightened, still standing on the sofa, when Qasim's voice rumbled out. She turned and found him just inside the office, leaning against the doorframe, hands hidden deep in the pockets of his dark trousers.

He appeared casual enough. His tie was discarded, and his collar was undone, revealing a glimpse of toned licorice skin. In spite of his cool, relaxed stance, Vectra wasn't deceived. It was all too easy to sense the man's ability to shift gears from relaxed to alert.

She'd dressed comfortably that day, choosing a simple mauve long-sleeved tunic dress. The frock easily transitioned to more business-appropriate attire with the addition of the matching high-heeled sandals that were currently under her desk. At that moment, however, Vectra felt decidedly underdressed.

Qasim left his spot at the door. "Your business manager let me in before she locked up."

Vectra smiled, aiming for easygoing instead of hot and bothered. "You *did* say nine." She glanced at the big-faced clock on a far wall of the office.

"So I did." Slowly, Qasim made his way toward where she stood barefoot in the middle of the sofa.

He stopped before her and took his time, raking his deep-set ebonies along her body. The dress, in no way clinging, did a superb job of showing off her very model-worthy legs, which he'd had the pleasure of feeling wrapped around his back many times the night before.

The intense throbbing and clenching she'd been riddled with at the start of her day returned with a vengeance. Vectra thought she had never felt so exposed, so eager.

She swallowed, following the reflex by clearing her throat. "I, um . . . I was just going to get my shoes."

He wouldn't let her pass when she moved. "What for?"

Vectra swallowed again. "I thought we were going out to dinner," she said quietly.

He touched her then, that beckoning stare of his fixed on the ascent of his fingers, grazing from just below her knee to where the hem of her dress ended several inches above.

"Did I say that?" he queried, mock confusion claiming his rich voice.

Vectra bit the corner of her bottom lip just after a moan betrayed her need. "You wanted to see me." She attempted to cover the slip by issuing the unnecessary reminder. The hand that had been riding the curve of her leg suddenly cupped her thigh.

"So I did," he admitted.

Her mind and body flooded with sensation, and she closed her eyes. Qasim tracked his other hand along her other leg and charted a path that bypassed the hem of her dress.

He didn't stop until he met the barrier of her panties. He cupped her crotch then and worked her scandalously beneath a wickedly talented thumb. Vectra couldn't have quieted her moans had she tried. Which she didn't.

Unsteady, she planted her hands on Qasim's shoulders, loving their unyielding width. She very much wanted to feel the sinewy muscle and perfect skin naked against her fingertips. Doing anything other than holding on for support was out of the question.

Ruthlessly, he tended to her clit, sending the nub of highly sensitized nerves into frenzy. The wide pad of his thumb made slow rotations clockwise and counter. He nuzzled his beautifully crafted face into her belly, breathing her in as he pleasured her and found his own in her reaction.

Vectra dug in her nails and arched toward the delicious things Qasim did beneath her dress. She could barely stand up straight and rocked insistently toward what his touch promised. She planted her knee against the upper quadrant of his chest, wanting to grant him as much access as he needed.

She was almost done for. She knew it. He hadn't even taken off her panties. She urged him on, her words slurred, practically indecipherable.

"Sim." The purr was low and needy. "I'm close . . . please . . . please don't let me come in my panties . . ."

His resulting laughter held a roguish element, and he didn't let up at all. Instead, he increased the pressure. His fingers ventured inside the crotch of her lingerie to test the merit of her fears. He sank into a pool of her cream and grinned. "Afraid it's a little too late for that."

Vectra didn't care. The dual massage of his thumb and middle finger had her selfishly fixated on reaching her peak. Sim thrust his finger high, driving and stirring her channel with repeated, maddening strokes. The moves had her sobbing as arousal and delight enveloped her in a cocoon of elation.

Shamelessly, she moved against him in a timeless rhythm until her body tensed in a telltale bow that prefaced deep shudders overtaking her slender frame.

"Good girl," Sim crooned, continuing his ruthless fingering and stroking as she came apart in his arms.

He was so thoroughly addicted to the way she sounded in the throes of ecstasy. She collapsed into him, but he could feel her muscles continuing to spasm around his finger.

He took pity then. Gently pulling her into his arms, Qasim kissed her temple and then placed her on the sofa. He went to retrieve her shoes from beneath the glass desk in the back of the office.

Returning to Vectra, he took the liberty of putting her into the strappy heels, massaging her calves once he was done.

"Are you upset with me?" An unapologetic smirk curved his kissable mouth.

"These are my favorite panties." She sounded playfully woeful and then sighed. "But that's what washing machines are for, right?"

Qasim reciprocated her shrug. "I know a place that's got a pretty good one."

"Really?"

"Mmm-hmm . . ."

Vectra pretended to ponder that. "I could use a nap, too."

"It's got a pretty amazing bed."

"Is that right? Good for sleeping?"

"Good for all kinds of things," he promised.

CHAPTER 11

Qasim found that Vectra wasn't teasing when she admitted to needing a nap. She dozed off after about ten minutes into their drive. She was out for the duration of the trip to his condo in Nob Hill, one of San Francisco's most coveted areas.

He didn't mind her sleeping. It gave him the chance to secure the SUV inside the private attached garage, take her into his arms and carry her inside. She stirred while he took a short stairway leading to the private elevator that opened right into the condo's living room.

"It's okay . . ." he soothed, "I've got you."

Vectra stirred again once the elevator car began its ascent.

"I've got you," he repeated and realized he wanted those words to ring true in every way that could matter. Leaning against the elevator's walnut-paneled walls, he rested his face into the top of her head and

171

breathed in the airy fragrance clinging to her short dark hair.

Vectra fidgeted once more. This time, she nuzzled her face near the collar of his shirt. He had covered her with his suit coat before taking her from the SUV. Qasim raised his head, tracing her features and appreciating the flawless appeal of her face. Hers was a face that, only in the security of his most secret thoughts, he would admit to wanting to wake up to every morning.

How would she feel about that? *Idiot.* She'd already given him that answer. Hadn't she? *I'm not a clingy woman,* she'd said.

Would she change her tune for the right man, he wondered. Could he get her to take a chance on him?

The car bumped softly upon reaching its destination and opened up in the living room. Qasim carried his alluring burden into his semidarkened retreat. Pausing for a time, he observed the dynamic view of the Bay and the sparkling lights of the city he adored. The view was visible from almost every one of the enormous windows, a prevalent feature of the condo's open floor plan that had moved Qasim to purchase it.

Quietly, he took the route to his bedroom across the rich, wide planks of the walnut floors. The condo was starkly designed, but

172

maintained unique warmth thanks to the towering bookcases and wide fireplaces in almost every room. Shallow, automatic lighting from the wardrobe room doused the bedroom when he arrived there with Vectra. He set her on the middle of the almond-colored comforter with its merlot-colored throw pillows cluttering the carved walnut headboard. He waited, ensuring the move hadn't jostled her awake. He moved to further dim the closet lighting.

With an expert touch, Qasim relieved Vectra of her shoes, dress and underthings. He got her situated between crisp, wine-colored sheets. All the while, he forbade himself to crawl in with her. Instead, he dutifully took her clothes to his laundry room. He made even more effective use of his time by going through the accumulated mail while the clothes washed and his house-guest slept.

Later, he returned, stripped and joined Vectra in bed, where he pulled her into a spooning embrace. Immediately, he was lulled to sleep by her radiant body, warm and pliant against him.

Vectra experienced a distinct sense of déjà vu when she woke in bed, and alone. Only this wasn't exactly déjà vu, she realized. It

173

wasn't morning. The room was dark with the exception of the lights sparkling in the far distance, and the sounds of the harbor were faint but noticeable.

She was also quite obviously not alone. She felt something warm and imposing between her legs. It obstructed her ability to close them. A sound, half sob, half moan, warbled from her throat when a heavy stab of pleasure radiated below her waist, turning her boneless with arousal.

"Sim." His name was distorted, given the sob-moan that continued to crowd her throat. The maddening throbbing and clenching that had plagued her all day resumed, and her hips began rocking slowly, keeping pace with the pleasurable drives from an all-too-skillful tongue.

A rough purr ventured upward through the sheets. Qasim had spent the past ten minutes relishing the task of waking her. Waking her in a truly ruthless manner, he admitted, but his desires had once again overruled his ability to practice any sort of bedroom etiquette.

He'd started by thumbing her labia. Every so often, he'd dip a finger inside her satin core until he'd found her very wet for him. Still, he'd resisted taking her until he'd known she was waking. He had pounced the moment he was sure she was lucid. Immersed in his task, he grunted consistent sounds of pure satisfaction at the discovery of finding her taste as addictive as her sounds of arousal when they reached his ears.

Vectra was close to orgasm, her wavering cries and quivering frame a testament to just how close she was.

"Not yet," Qasim ordered, smirking briefly when she sobbed her disappointment. He held her thighs trapped, arms enfolding each of the lush, caramel-toned limbs to keep her virtually immobile. He only allowed for the minute rise, fall and rotation of her hips as she reacted to every lick and thrust from his tongue.

Vectra reached for him, needing to cling to his shoulders or rake her nails through the close-cut silk of his hair. She could find no physical purchase on the monstrous bed. There was no mistaking the fact that he was there, though.

Teetering recklessly on the edge of climax, one she was forbidden to give in to, Vectra smoothed her hands over her body. Fleetingly, she flicked her nipples beneath her thumbnails and then raked her fingers through her hair.

"Sim!" His name was a moan-gasp that

tumbled forth while she eagerly rode his tongue.

The need to sob, full and unabashed, crashed in when he ceased his attentions inside her core and rained erotic torment upon her clit. His tongue coursed over the sensitive nub, and then his lips sucked there at length. Abundant joy sent Vectra shuddering on the cusp of an insane release.

"No, Vectra."

"Sim, please . . . please let me. Sim . . ."

He took pity. Some.

Vectra labeled it as some new form of torture when he simply denied her his touch. She lashed out, making weak contact with the iron slab of muscle comprising a formidable bicep.

"Sim —" Her mouth was suddenly filled with his tongue that had been handling her so stunningly.

Vectra forgot her sensual misery and showed her approval by languidly massaging his tongue with hers. Ravenously, she suckled, loving how she tasted on his mouth.

"Sim, please . . . I can't . . . wait," she shared during the kiss.

Qasim understood, unable to deny himself anymore either. He was painfully hard and throbbing for her. Covering her body with his, Qasim truly feared he was done for. Her silken body threatened to send him right over an unforgiving edge.

He groped across the bed, scouring the area for the condoms he'd tossed there when he'd awakened to find her still dozing next to him. Need returned in a blaze that hadn't been totally doused, but simply put on hold during his time away from her. He snagged one of the packets and tore his mouth from hers to rip into the packet with his teeth.

Vectra accepted the break in their kiss and used the time to drag her tongue up the strong, corded column of his throat, pausing to nibble his earlobe. Then it was Qasim who was begging.

He applied protection, cursing fiercely until he'd completed the job. Then, he took her in one swift, beautiful progression. Their coupling adopted a wild tempo from the onset. Vectra didn't hold back, shuddering her pleasure into the dark expanse of the room. Qasim drew one of her calves across his shoulder as he pounded into her, bringing along an onslaught of superb sensation.

Vectra met the power of his thrusts with a brand all her own. She feared it would be another seductive round he'd win until he suddenly flipped her and took her from behind. Bracing on all fours, she accepted him. Her energy was renewed by the slow, deep, filling strokes that awakened some new spot he had just discovered.

"Vectra." Qasim spoke her name each time he slid home to be gloved inside her. He'd wanted her for so long and had imagined so many ways of taking her, ways upon ways that had been paired and then shifted in such a way that it would take an eternity to experience them all.

He wanted to pace himself, but she made that impossible.

"Sim . . ."

He crouched closer, caging her. "Come for me."

The request had a shattering effect on Vectra. Quivering, she gave in to the feelings his body inside hers had given her. She felt his hand flex almost painfully on her hip as his own release erupted. She felt his seed filling the condom, and she reflexively clenched. Her walls milked his sex until he was the one gasping for reprieve.

The lovers remained locked in their embrace for a long while before either felt like breaking the bond. When they did, it was to reclaim the sweet spooning embrace they had started the night with.

Dawn made its appearance in subtle fashion

178

that morning. Vectra snuggled in closer to the heated wall that was Qasim's chest. She smiled, soothed by the sound of rain tapping the expansive windows that comprised an entire side of the bedroom.

The day was slated to be a dreary one, but the overcast weather had no effect on Vectra. Contentment ruled her, and she was happy to let it take the lead. The strong, dependable beat of Qasim's heart had lulled her to sleep once he'd drawn her back next to him, and its arousing rhythm thudded through her.

They had changed positions during the few hours of sleep that had followed the rapacious love scene that had begun during the morning's wee hours. Vectra woke with his chest pillowing her head, and she wished they could spend the day that way.

Qasim must have felt the same. He stirred when she wriggled against him.

He pressed his face to the top of her head. "Will you stay with me today?"

Vectra bit her lip, secreting away the happiness brightening her face. "Don't you have billions to make for someone today?" She heard him laugh and gave in to a bit of girlish lash-fluttering over the sound.

"I made everybody their billions yesterday," he said.

"In that case, I'd be thrilled to lounge the day away with you."

"Who said anything about lounging?"

Qasim hoisted her up, and Vectra found herself lying flush against him. Her heart jumped into her throat, but she managed to swallow around it. "Your stamina is unreal."

He cupped the back of her head, brushing his thumb through her clipped, sleek locks. "It's all natural."

Vectra didn't doubt the boast, but she didn't have time to share that. He was occupying her mouth with his sinful, skillful tongue.

She moaned, returning the slow swirls he used to entice a response she was all too willing to give. Without hesitation, her tongue tangled with his, and she synced her tongue thrusts with his. When she felt his engorged sex insistently nudging her inner thighs, she instantly gasped, giving him leave to deepen their lusty kiss.

Sensuously slow, she writhed against him, slowing once her core aligned with his iron thickness. She whimpered over the sheer satisfaction he was capable of providing with that part of his anatomy.

A low sound of lurking promise rushed heat through her extremities and robbed her of any teasing intent. Hungrily, she crested her palms along the taut, licorice muscle of his amazing chest and abdomen.

Using the granite slab of his torso for leverage, Vectra pushed into a sitting position. Straddling his lap as she was sent shudders through her body. Rippling throbs came next, a direct result of his erection nudging her entrance.

Qasim caught her hips. He primed her with a few warning squeezes, the last of which he used to lift her up, only to ease her back down to sit on his massive upper thighs. A few more of those enticing nudges and he'd be sinking his bare sex inside hers.

He reached beneath the pillow cradling his head, located a condom, tore into the packet and set it in place.

Then he claimed her.

Vectra found she was too passion drunk from sensation to do much more than cling to him for purchase.

Qasim had no problem taking command of their encounter. Maneuvering her svelte body only required trace amounts of his considerable strength. Grabbing her hips, he lowered and lifted her to his satisfaction, grunting each time she sheathed him in a tight, warm haven of cream.

Vectra swayed and rotated her hips, her body wrought with elation. She could feel him tense in the telltale sign that prefaced release.

The pressure increased against her walls. She threw back her head, her voice hoarse from the many times she'd cried out her enjoyment that morning.

Once Qasim had spent himself, she collapsed upon his chest. The sounds of their breathing mingled with the rain.

Later that morning, Vectra, still in Qasim's bed, spoke with her gallery manager, Katherine Wiseman. "Everything's fine, Kate. I didn't leave the gallery 'til late, so I decided to grab a hotel room. I took a cab instead of driving."

"Excellent idea." Kate's slightly nasal tone of voice rang with approval. "Taking a day for yourself — at long last."

Vectra smiled, scooting deeper into the bed. "Glad you approve."

"Well, we've got everything under control, so all will be well in time for the showing."

"Hide the Croachman canvas." Vectra arched up suddenly upon remembering the piece. "I swear it, Kate. Somebody's gonna lose a hand if they try to take it from me."

Kate dissolved into waves of laughter. "Got it!"

The call ended shortly after and in time

for Qasim's return to the bedroom suite. He brought with him a tray teeming with food. Vectra, garbed in the shirt Qasim had worn the day before, scooted up to her knees in the bed. She moved over to make room for him to place the tray to the middle of the rumpled covers.

In spite of the incredible smells wafting from the tray, her focus lingered on the raw masculinity he exuded. He was clothed only in a pair of gray sleep pants slung low on his hips. His sleek chest was left perfectly bare and mouthwatering.

"Dive in," he urged.

"I commend you on your hospitality." Vectra leaned closer to take in the delectable offerings. "I see why your love life is so successful if every woman you entertain gets the same treatment."

Qasim stilled, having just grabbed a piece of banana bread. "Who said I have a successful love life?"

Does the man even own a mirror? Vectra shook her head, still not suspecting there was anything amiss in his question. "Any woman with eyes can see you have a successful love life," she said.

"I'm guessing there's a compliment in there somewhere?"

Blinking, her mouth full of bacon, Vectra's

expression cleared. "Did I offend you?"

"I'm just not real high on being called a slut." He shrugged.

Vectra gaped and then gave into unrestrained laughter when he followed up the shrug with a sly wink.

Once the laughter settled into comfortable silence, they focused on the breakfast Qasim had prepared. They had been eating a while before he spoke again.

"This is my home, Vectra. I've never brought another woman here."

This time she stilled. She watched him wolf down his food, curiosity waging war on her body temperature.

So why did he bring me here?

She didn't dare ask that question aloud.

He'd already told her he was possessive when it came to her. Did that possession go beyond the act of sexual claiming? She swallowed her bacon and the corner of a biscuit with sincere effort.

Qasim scarfed down several more large portions of his food. "You want to know why I brought you, right?"

"Well —" she smiled, intending to make light of the matter "— we're both well-known." She popped a grape into her mouth, chewed around it. "Between trying to keep my well-meaning but nosy staff

184

clueless and making sure we aren't spotted at an area hotel, your place offers us the most privacy."

Qasim stopped eating. His pitch-black gaze glinted with shards of frustration. "Do you think that's why I brought you here?"

"Not entirely." She could see that he didn't appreciate the answer. "It's a reasonable motivation, Qasim."

"Is that easier for you to handle? That I brought you here because it was convenient?"

She gave him the benefit of an unapologetic stare. "I know what this is, and I told you I was fine with it. I meant that." To herself she confided that she wasn't too happy about making a point of it.

She wanted more than the physical act of sex. She wanted the tenderness, the sharing and the man far beyond the time limit that a fling allowed. Would he welcome that knowledge? Vectra accepted the fact that she just wasn't willing to reveal that much of her hand.

"Are you telling me that's not it?" She tried to determine whether he'd reveal more of his own.

"I won't deny that I value my privacy. It's something that I had very little of growing up. Hmph — very little? Try none. The foster care system doesn't care much for providing homes promising areas for quiet reflection." He smiled, but it didn't quite reach his eyes. "I'm telling you that I didn't want anyone interrupting what I wanted to do with you last night and that I have thought about doing that to you here in my bed for a very long time."

"Oh." She swallowed on the word.

Qasim quietly celebrated the fact that he'd pretty much rendered her speechless. There was more he wanted to confess, but he could be patient until she was ready to hear it. Despite her open, carefree demeanor, he sensed that she would be very cautious going into her next involvement. The last thing he wanted to do was pressure her. She'd had enough of that.

Qasim's eyes roamed the tempting length of her legs all the way to her exquisite face. He wondered at what was going on behind those lovely features — how was she really reacting to what he had confessed? She seemed entranced by her food, apparently not wanting to delve any further into the topic.

"Eat up." He smiled. "You're gonna need your strength." He heard her quiet moan escape her and his smile deepened.

CHAPTER 12

Qasim returned Vectra to the gallery the next morning. Their day together had been beyond anything Vectra had ever experienced. She admitted to feeling a little like a virgin — *post*virginity. Her cheeks actually burned over memories of things done . . . and undone.

Her fingers brushed the back of his hand, halting its slow progress beneath her dress when he reached across the gear shift. They would be working on day two of their lovers' tryst if she let his touch roam any higher.

The possibility of that did nothing to diminish her participation in the kiss they shared. Moaning as though overcome by thirst, Vectra desperately engaged his tongue.

Qasim knew he was playing with fire. It was a habit he was growing quite fond of. Sadly, it was not the right time or place. He wasn't of a mind to take her on the front seat of his truck, regardless of how much the idea appealed to him.

"Take you inside?"

She smiled, loving the sensation of his velvety soft lips murmuring against hers. She inched back, though, as far as he'd allow, and scanned the street where the gallery was located.

She could see the movers carting in canvases of Yancey Croachman's work and recognized the cars of her staff along the hilly street.

"It's all right," she said. "The place is already jumping."

"How long will you be here?" Qasim cast a dark look toward the gallery entrance.

"Not long. I only need to get my car and then I'll probably work from my dad's place here in the city." She smoothed a wispy lock behind her ear. "We're supposed to have lunch together, and I'll be able to grab a change of clothes there without having to drive back out to the vineyard."

"Can I see you tonight?"

She melted. "When do you want me to come over?"

Qasim didn't miss how quickly she'd mentioned driving herself. "I'll pick you up from your dad's."

"Qasim, I really don't mind —"

"I'll see you at eight." He reached out to wind a clipped lock of her hair about his middle finger. He dropped another kiss to her mouth, a sweet one that left her hungry for more, and then he shifted to leave the SUV.

She realized his intention to escort her and grabbed his arm. "Qasim, it's okay."

He didn't argue and knew the muscle he could feel flexing along his jawline was all too noticeable. It was a dead giveaway to how valiantly he worked to tether his agitation over her refusal.

Vectra noticed, however. She leaned across the gear console to smooth the back of her hand across the silken whiskers that shaded his cheek.

"It's all right. It's safe." Intentionally she downplayed what he was really agitated about. "It's practically a full house in there," she added.

"Get out of here before I change my mind," he said, his tone gruff yet playful.

"I'll see you tonight." She smiled encouragingly and then left the vehicle under her own steam.

When she was gone, Qasim shrugged a clenched fist to his thigh.

"Easy, Sim." He sighed.

Vectra saw to a few things at the gallery. Her staff was used to finding her in clothes from the previous day when she put in one of her late-night work sessions, so there was no questioning her attire. She then headed off to her father's place.

Oscar Bauer had decided to return to his roots and had opted for a three-story loft in SoMa.

Short for *South of Market,* SoMa was known for its artsy cultural appeal. Vectra believed it was the place that had sparked her love for art and the gallery scene. After his wife's death, Oscar no longer felt comforted by the quiet captivation of Carro and the memories of his beloved mate.

Vectra had always enjoyed trips to the city to visit her father's eclectic stomping grounds. Yet when Oscar decided to move back into the area, both Vectra and Oliver had been more than a little concerned. They admitted to being unable to picture their dad living amidst such energy.

They had little to fear. Oscar had settled in nicely and had selected a terrific place to do it.

The loft was a uniquely crafted dwelling.

Despite its open floor plan, the place was chock-full of cozy nooks and crannies furnished with overstuffed chairs and sofas. Rejuvenating natural illumination poured through skylights and a roof that had been the scene for many unforgettable barbecues. Oscar Bauer, however, spent a great deal of his time on the lofty third level, which comprised his home office suite. Vectra usually had the run of the place whenever she visited. Her father's office/man cave held relatively everything he needed, which made Oscar comfortable leaving his daughter to her own devices in the rest of the house.

Such was the case that morning when Vectra arrived.

"Dad?!"

"Up here, baby!"

"Figures! Don't come down!" Vectra laughed, genuinely pleased to find him at work — or play — in his private domain. In truth, she wasn't much in the mood to explain why she was there for a change of clothes.

Not that her father ever questioned such things. Like her house staff, he'd probably throw a party if he knew her reason had to do with a man. Qasim Wilder, at that. Oscar had made no secret of how much he approved of the successful investment broker.

Vectra took her coffee from the sunlit second level kitchen and headed over to enjoy it from the attached alcove. The space offered an excellent view of the culturally energetic area. Its vibrancy was evident even during daylight hours. Still, her thoughts returned to Qasim.

Returned? Hmph, they were never far away from him. That was especially true now that their relationship had transcended into the lovers' realm. He'd been upset when they parted ways earlier that morning. She knew it and didn't find fault in his reaction. Twice, she'd refused him. The actions surprised her. She had no explanation for it. Part of her wanted to shout to anyone who'd listen that she was floating on a cloud and Qasim was the reason.

The other part of her wanted no one to know, fearing what they'd found was something that would not last. Worse, she'd be to blame for it. Residual baggage from her previous relationship disaster wasn't her excuse. At least, not fully. The experience, however, had rendered her much more cautious with her heart.

Or . . . she thought it had. She really wanted to serve her heart to Qasim Wilder on a platter with all the trimmings. Unfortunately, caution had been her game for so long that she wasn't sure how to shake it. All the while, her instincts were screaming that playing it safe wasn't warranted.

"Vecs!" her father called down. It was then that she tuned in to the doorbell's chimes. Quickly, she set aside her coffee and rushed for the boxed wooden staircase that would take her down to the main level.

"Got it, Dad!" she called on her way down. Within seconds, she was opening the front door to someone she wouldn't have expected, but was pleased to see.

"Vectra, thank God." Minka Gerald appeared more relieved than pleased.

"Minka? You okay?" Concern heightened, Vectra pulled the woman inside with a tug to her elbow.

"Sorry for the theatrics, I —" Minka paused to inhale a calming breath. "I went to see you at the gallery, but your staff said you were working from here today."

"Why didn't you just call me?" Vectra steered the woman deeper inside the loft.

Minka shook her head and gave a mystified shrug. "I'm not working on all cylinders today."

"This calls for tea," Vectra said, guiding them back toward the staircase.

"Incredible." Minka inhaled again, taking

the time to observe her surroundings. "I heard your dad had some place."

"Yeah —" Vectra laughed "— he doesn't laze about in it as much as I do, though. Keeps to his office." She looked toward the ceiling and huffed.

They made it up to the second level. There, Minka went wild over the stunning view. Mirrors practically walled the wide open space. Smaller picture windows filled the chrome-and-granite kitchen while wider ones lined the alcove and enclosed the dining room on three sides.

Vectra set a shiny black kettle to boil. "So why isn't your brain working on all cylinders?" she asked.

Minka set her wrap and tote bag to the dark gray tiled kitchen island and sighed. "It's probably got a lot to do with the fact that I've drained a great deal of its power into investigating a coworker."

"Are you sure, Mink? This is serious stuff."

"You're tellin' *me*?" Minka gulped down more of the herbal blend she'd been guzzling while relaying her suspicions of Will Lloyd's embezzlement of funds from the Wilder Warriors Foundation.

"I went home the night before thinking I was the worst kind of person for snooping into something like this and then I come back to work yesterday knowing I *had* to snoop into it." Minka leaned forward, pressing the backs of her hands against her eyes and shaking her head. "Thank God Sim decided to take yesterday off."

Vectra cleared her throat and poured a third cup of the wonderful-smelling blend. "Minka . . . why are you telling me this? I mean, isn't there a rule against spilling company secrets?"

Minka rolled her eyes. "I'm not sure if Qasim had this type of thing in mind when he helped set the company bylaws."

"From what I hear, he's a great boss. You should talk to him."

Minka gaped. "Are you crazy?" She moved to reach for her mug then squeezed her hands closed when she saw how badly they were shaking. "I mean, did you *hear* all Will's war stories the other night? The man saved Qasim's life. My guess is it'd be pretty hard to believe anything bad about someone who did that, you know?"

"So what are you gonna do?" Vectra studied the pattern she tapped out around the mouth of her mug.

"I'm doing it. I'm asking *you* to talk to Qasim."

"Are you crazy?" Vectra bolted from the

deep Queen Anne chair she occupied in the alcove where they enjoyed the tea.

Minka had grown utterly calm. "He'll listen to you, Vectra."

"How do you figure?"

"He's in love with you."

Vectra returned to the chair with a hard bounce. "How do you know that?"

"Anyone with eyes would know that."

Vectra blinked, absorbing the other woman's words.

"Minka, listen." Vectra smoothed her hands along the chair arms. "Most men don't like it when people meddle in their business. Especially women they . . . love."

"He's got to be told." Minka leaned forward in the matching Queen Anne, extending her hands in a needy display. "I've already put my foot in my mouth and made Will look bad when we were debating over the hotels. Qasim might see this as a petty attempt to get something started."

"You're his assistant, Mink. He counts on you to point out when he's making stupid business decisions."

"Once bitten, twice shy."

Minka's simple defense drained Vectra's will to argue. After all, Vectra thought, hadn't she been battling with the same line in defense of her own actions?

"Would you just think about it?" Minka pleaded.

Think about it? Sure. Think about repeating an act that had once opened the doorway to an abusive relationship?

No problem.

Vectra groaned, hiding her face in her palms.

"I told you I love it, Dad."

"But you've only seen it on paper." Oscar Bauer closed the leather portfolio that carried information about his intended real estate acquisition in Lake Misurina, Italy.

Vectra patted her father's hand over the portfolio. "If *you* love it, then I love it. Who am I to throw in my two cents about a place you want as your retirement oasis?"

Oscar's square jaw clenched. "You're my daughter *and,*" he emphasized when Vectra opened her mouth to reply, "the closest thing I have to your mother. Having you go there and give your blessing would be like having her do it. In *my* mind, anyway."

Vectra's smile was indulgent as she squeezed her dad's hand. "This is unfair, but too sweet to refuse."

He grinned. "Pleased I've persuaded you."

"But I don't think Oliver would be too happy to hear you say *I'm* the closest thing you have to Momma."

"Hmph." Oscar bumped his fist lightly against Vectra's jaw. "My son is a handsome devil, but I know he'd agree he's nowhere near as beautiful as you are."

"That's what *you* think!"

Father and daughter shared a laugh at Oliver's expense and continued their lunch at the small but popular bar and grill not far from Oscar's SoMa loft. When Vectra heard her dad chuckle out Qasim's name, her gaze flew upward to lock with his bottomless ebony stare.

"Mr. B." Qasim greeted the older man with a handshake.

"Join us, kid!" Oscar urged.

"I'll have to decline this time, sir."

"What are you doing here?" Vectra blurted, dismissing the shivers attacking her beneath the cotton fabric of her olive-green wrap dress.

Qasim appeared pleased by her curiosity. "I had a meeting with a client."

"We need to get together, too, Sim. My treat," Oscar offered.

Qasim chuckled. "I never turn down a free lunch. We'll make it happen soon." He returned his focus to Vectra and then, holding her gaze, he leaned down to apply a lingering kiss to her cheek. "I'll see you tonight." He made no attempt to whisper.

Vectra waited for the floor to open up and swallow her.

Qasim straightened. "Have a good day, sir." He nodded to Oscar and moved on.

Oscar's expression had gone from curious, to stunned, to elated in a matter a seconds. He steadied his voice in hopes of keeping those very visible emotions from betraying him to his daughter, however. "It'd be a good idea for you to bring him with you to Italy."

"Dad!" Vectra was utterly floored.

Oscar shrugged. "What? It makes perfect sense. I trust Sim to tell me if I'm making good investments."

"And what about all that 'your blessing is all I need' stuff?"

Oscar shrugged again. "I need *your* spiritual blessing and Sim's financial. See? All my bases are covered."

Vectra couldn't help but laugh.

"I won't apologize for today." Qasim wasn't surprised by Vectra's unexpected arrival at his place that night earlier than he'd planned. But if he was honest, he'd actually counted on her showing up right after lunch.

"Do you think I expect an apology?" she asked.

"Don't you?"

"Does my answer determine admittance?"

Qasim stepped aside, silently admitting her to move forward. "Did Oscar ask questions?" he asked.

"No . . ." Vectra's tone was deceptively airy. "He really didn't have to since you pretty much gave him all the answers."

Grinning, Qasim closed the door and followed her inside the condo. "Is that a problem for you?"

She strolled the walnut flooring, her spiky sandals lightly clicking in her wake. "If it were a problem, I'd have come here demanding an apology."

"Demanding," Qasim repeated the word while stalking her around the open main room.

"I'd be well within my rights."

"Would you, now?"

"Very well within . . . I'm just not all that fond of my dad being 'in the know' about my sex life."

"Understood." Qasim gave in to soft laughter. "But in my defense, the man did look very happy."

Vectra cringed. "Could we just *not* talk about it?"

She turned to resume her trek around the inviting room and Qasim resumed his prowl behind her. "I'm good with not talking."

Vectra heard him impossibly close behind her. She turned in time to find herself against the side of one of the towering bookcases in the living room doorway.

Qasim dipped his head, at the same time trailing his hand down the soft fabric of Vectra's dress. Then, he tugged up her thigh, hugging it against his hip.

Vectra sealed herself against him, rolling her hips until she was perfectly aligned with his shaft. The organ had rapidly made the transition from semi to rock-hard beneath the fine material of his sandalwood-colored trousers. Eagerly, she angled her head and outlined the felt-smooth curve of his mouth with the tip of her tongue.

Her tentative initiation of the kiss was drowned beneath a robust growl that did weird things to her stomach. The erotic roll of her hips became more insistent, a grind that rubbed her clit along the ridge of his sex. The action sent explosive spasms through her core.

Qasim showed mercy, massaging the hand that supported her thigh against his hip. Strong fingers walked the length of the limb until they brushed the middle of her lace panties.

She shuddered in reaction and welcomed the new layer of pleasure. Their kiss became throatier. His tongue worked feverishly inside her mouth as if to slake a deep-seated lust. Vectra loosed faint, tortured whimpers and met Qasim's demanding kiss with her own. Her nails raked the crisp whiskers shading his jaw.

Vectra was so absorbed in the kiss that she lost track of what his skillful fingers were doing. She flinched when one breached the quivering folds of her sex.

Qasim suddenly broke the kiss, sharp curiosity sweltering in his midnight stare. "What?" he probed.

"Sorry."

"Did I hurt you?"

"No, Sim —"

"Have I been hurting you, V?" He tilted his head, lowering it just a fraction in order to look at her more directly.

A delighted chill countered the heat that had been ravishing Vectra when he shortened her name. Qasim squeezed her thigh, giving it a gentle jerk that centered her.

"Just tender." She let him see her discomfort over the admission. "It had been a while, a long while. Years . . ." she confessed.

He grinned, the action narrowing his gaze and accentuating the draw of his dark eyes. "That's got to be the best thing I've heard in a long time."

"Hmph." She wasn't convinced. "Trust me when I say it sounds way better than it feels."

Qasim let her thigh slip away from his hip but kept her close to his chest in order to lift her until she was at his eye level.

"Let's eat," he suggested.

Vectra refused to budge. "Did I turn you off?"

His thumb skirted her cheek and the curve of her mouth. "You'd laugh if you knew how impossible it'd be for you to do that." He pressed his forehead to hers.

"Sim?" He still had her confused.

"I've been wanting to ask whether I was hurting you for a while now."

"And you didn't, because?" She sounded as if she knew the answer.

His lashes fluttered as though he were aggravated with himself. "I didn't want you to think I was asking because I was hung up on what happened to you."

"But aren't you?"

"Damn right, I am." His voice was a sim-mering growl that dripped with menacing promise. "It'd make me very happy to have a few moments alone with your ex." He squeezed his eyes shut in an effort to stifle the rage beginning its slow rumble in his gut.

He focused. "We've, um . . . we've been going at it pretty steady for the last few days. You haven't complained, but I–I wondered."

Her smile was naughtiness and satisfaction. "I didn't complain because I had no complaints. I wanted this, and you gave me exactly what I wanted."

Vectra's warm brown eyes narrowed, her expression sharpening with wickedly playful intent. "If you apologize for that or even *think* about tamping down any of that amazing stamina of yours, I'll seriously consider murdering you."

Qasim's dark eyes crinkled adorably as his laughter built. It burst forth, full and honest, as he nodded his acceptance.

"So?" He pulled her higher up his arms and led the way to the dining room. "Supper and then sex?"

"Mmm . . ." Vectra scrunched her nose. "I'm not too wild about that sequence."

Qasim nodded and deftly shifted direction toward his bedroom. "Whatever the lady wants."

CHAPTER 13

The next few days were full of more of the delicious same for Qasim and Vectra. Holed up in his gorgeous condo, the new lovers found it difficult to tear themselves away from each other and what was growing between them.

Nonetheless, the outside world *did* call. Wilder Corporation ran so successfully because of Qasim's hands-on manner of managing his clients' individual needs. He would've been happier tending his duties had he been able to convince Vectra to stay where she was and to be there in his bed when he got back.

Spending time in San Francisco wouldn't raise much suspicion. Vectra's house staff knew she tended to do that when she was preparing for an opening. Vectra would've liked nothing more than to oblige Qasim's request, but duty called for her, as well.

She had taken an obvious liking to Yancey

Croachman and knew it had a lot to do with the fact that she and the woman shared horrifically similar experiences. In spite of that, Yancey had risen above it all and she was thriving. Vectra, however, wanted to do more than simply buy a painting, and she actually patted herself on the back when what she knew was a brilliant idea occurred. She'd spoken to the marketing group for Carro as well as Robb DeWitt and his crew at Dazzles. Everyone thought that using Yancey Croachman's show would be the perfect event to unveil the vineyard's new blends.

By including the tasting, they could judge the crowd's reactions to the premiere wines while plying them with treasured favorites from the line. The event was sure to draw an even greater crowd than the gallery event alone would.

Vectra believed the young artist being showcased would make out splendidly with offers for more work and gallery tours. The artist herself was elated by the news as was the rest of her team. Vectra only prayed the showing would be as successful in reality as the one she imagined.

Of course not all of the time the new lovers enjoyed was spent in the bedroom. Vectra had heard much about Qasim's charity, but realized she had no clue about what had inspired it. Something told her it was about more for him than wanting to give back. The extent to which he'd crafted his foundation came from a much more personal place.

"He's out here somewhere, Ms. Bauer."

Despite the white sun visor she wore, Vectra squinted out over the football field that surged with activity. Minipractice sessions took place across every square foot of the lush hundred-yard field.

"I'll go track him down," said Jerry Finch, assistant coach for the Arnold High School Bears.

Vectra touched the man's arm to stop him. "Oh, don't go to all that trouble. I already texted him that I was on my way. I don't mind waiting." She smiled toward the field. "I haven't been this close to the game in a while."

"You like football?" Jerry cocked a brow, appearing doubtful.

Vectra took no offense to the way the man eyed her. She realized she looked more the part of rich heiress than pigskin enthusiast, dressed as she was in a sporty-chic tan tennis skirt, matching top and pristine white sneaker-clogs.

"I haven't had much time to enjoy it lately," she told the coach.

Jerry chuckled, and his pale blues twinkled in contrast against a healthy tan. "Don't worry, hanging around Qasim will change all that."

Vectra noticed the man raised his head in a quick up-and-down move, and she followed the line of his gaze to find Qasim heading toward them at a light jog.

"Sim!" Jerry called. "Looks like you've got a football lover on your hands."

Qasim grinned. "So she says."

Jerry and Vectra both laughed.

"Have you guys met?" Qasim asked.

"Oh, yes, Jerry showed me in," Vectra explained.

"I'll leave you guys to it," Jerry said and then tipped the brim of his cap emblazoned with the Bears' mascot. "Enjoy yourself, Ms. Bauer."

"Thanks, Jerry." Vectra smiled.

"Sim." The coach nodded and then jogged away.

Turning back to Qasim, Vectra acted out a playful cringe. "Will you try to break the man in half later for escorting me to the field?"

"Hmm . . ." Qasim made a pretense of considering the idea, and then shook his head. "Nah . . . Jerry's an all right guy. Besides, he's married."

She laughed. "So married men are safe?"

Qasim shrugged as though accepting the observation as fact. Inwardly, though, he felt a measure of accomplishment. He'd experienced none of the lightning-fast possessiveness that had been jolting through him with such annoying frequency over the thought of another man touching her. Deciding he deserved a treat for his progress, Sim turned the brim of his cap backward and drew Vectra high against him for a thorough kiss.

"There're kids present," she reminded him while arching into his chest.

" 'S all right. It'll give 'em somethin' to strive for."

Vectra would have laughed, but her mouth was quickly occupied by another probing kiss. When applause and whistles reached their ears, she felt her cheeks burn. She buried her face in Qasim's neck. Meanwhile, Qasim grinned and tipped his cap to the Arnold Bears Football Organization.

"It's amazing that you're able to send all these kids to college," Vectra raved, her warm stare trekking across the activity-rich field. She and Qasim enjoyed the rest of the

preseason practice from the stadium bleach-
ers.

"Well —" he grinned somewhat bashfully
"— I don't send *all,* only the ones whose
GPAs are a certain level. I'd love it if they
all made it to the pros, but it'd be better for
my wallet if their skills brought them to
work for me."

"Ah." Vectra laughed. "So you're trying to
scout mini-Wilders, huh?"

"I like that." He seemed to purr and then
shrugged. "My goal is just to help 'em suc-
ceed. College isn't for everyone, and I've
insisted that foundation money offers help
in whatever way the older kids require."

"Your dedication is commendable." Vectra
squinted, not in reaction to the sun but to
veil the hint of unease that talk of the
foundation had triggered in her eyes.

It had been several days since her chat
with Minka. Vectra was no closer to talking
with Qasim about the woman's concerns.
She didn't even know if she *wanted* to talk
to him about them.

"You've started something really wonder-
ful here, Qasim. You should be proud," she
said instead. "What was the inspiration? Did
some mysterious benefactor give you *your*
start in life?"

"Nah." He chuckled, watching his hands

while he rubbed them one inside the other. "I was a player but didn't have the desire to continue school beyond what the law required." He shook his head.

"My tune changed after the army. *That* was my benefactor, and I've never regretted the choice. I just want these kids to have another one. Kids from other backgrounds have them, why shouldn't these?"

"What you do is amazing," Vectra squeezed his arm. "A lot of people think so."

It was true. The Wilder Warriors Foundation had gained praise from many quarters on a national scale and had even grabbed attention at the presidential level.

"Has it always run so smoothly?" She studied the hub of activity on the field. "I know how easily charities can see their fair share of drama."

"You're right, and I'm happy we haven't." His hands curved into fists that he clenched and unclenched. "The person who dares to betray us would spend the rest of their lives regretting it."

"Jail?"

"If necessary. But I wouldn't want to make a public issue of it, if I could help it. Anyone that'd deny a kid the chance to make a life for himself deserves to have his own livelihood screwed with."

Vectra appeared impressed by his shrewd ability. "Remind me never to get on your bad side."

"Count on it." He grinned.

They were sealing the promise with a handshake when a stream of whistles blew to signal the end of practice.

CHAPTER 14

One week later

Guests filed into Gallery V on plush red carpeting that trailed out from the establishment's towering glass-encased pine doors. Black velvet ropes lined the carpet and were supported by gleaming silver stanchions.

Just inside the grand, split-level gallery, showing attendees were treated to a glass of their favorite Carro Vineyards wine. They were also informed of the exclusive tasting event that would occur following remarks from the gallery's owner, Vectra Bauer.

Vectra always experienced a burst of positive energy during every show. That was especially true for the artists who were relatively new to the scene. She loved the idea of having a part to play in the career of a new and intriguing creator. Vectra had a feeling that Yancey Croachman would be such a person.

Making her way across the gallery's gleaming marble floors, Vectra was a vision in a curve-adoring silk creation. The ankle-length skirt was overlaid in chiffon and carried a deep side split that flashed show-stopping glimpses of leg and thigh with each step she took.

It was never a chore to mingle, but never before had Qasim Wilder been a guest. It was all Vectra could do to keep her mind on her business and off her man. A genuine smile curved her mouth when she accepted a glass of moscato from a passing waiter.

Her man . . . She *did* like the sound of that. Sipping the flavorful wine that was just a bit too fruity for her taste, Vectra scanned the crowd. She stopped when she found what she searched for. Qasim stood on the gallery's main floor where he talked with Robb DeWitt and the man's head bartender, Joy Aiden.

Yes, Vectra thought, she did like the idea of Qasim Wilder being her man.

Only to herself would she dare admit to how much she'd liked the idea of him being *more* than her man. She could feel a swoon on the way, her body riddled with throbbing arousal. This, despite the fact that she'd just had the pleasure of the man less than twenty-four hours earlier.

Eyes off the candy, Vec.

She shook her head and turned, smiling at the sight of Minka Gerald. The woman made her way up the curving glass staircase to the second floor.

"Minka?" Vectra greeted with a smile and quick hug when they met just off the landing. "Now, what's wrong with this picture?" She pretended to ponder and then snapped her fingers. She took a glass of wine from another passing tray and presented it to Minka with a flourish.

Minka sipped, but didn't appear pleased.

"Please try to enjoy yourself," Vectra urged.

"Have you made up your mind about talking to Qasim?" Minka countered.

"Minka —"

"You have to, Vectra. It's above my head to do anything about it now."

Vectra stilled. "What do you mean?"

"Will's here." Minka's dark gaze skirted the room. "He's been waiting on paperwork that'll give him the power to sign off on virtually anything having to do with the charity that requires Sim's signature. I've been stalling, and he's suspicious. Somehow, he's figured out what I've been up to — says he'll go to Sim and have me fired if I say anything."

215

"He can't do that, Minka." Vectra squeezed the woman's arm reassuringly. "Qasim trusts you."

Minka was shaking her head. "I can't take that chance . . ." Her gaze fell when Vectra moved closer.

"What'd he say to you? Exactly? Minka, did he threaten you?" Vectra asked when the woman offered no response to her two prior questions.

"He . . ."

"Minka?"

"He's too smart for that." Minka smirked. "He was one I seriously underestimated."

"Talk to Sim," Vectra urged.

"And what if he doesn't believe me?" Minka's gaze hardened in tandem with her voice. "I'll have to deal with Will *and* the fact that I ruined a friendship that means a lot to Qasim."

"I don't think you believe that." Vectra could see, though, that Minka had strong reason to believe the worst of his old army buddy. She liked Minka too much to let her think she had nowhere to turn.

"I give it a month."

Qasim grinned when he heard Robb's prediction. "Until?" he asked.

"You ask that girl to marry you."

216

"You're forgetting my possessiveness issues."

"I don't buy it." Robb waved off the reminder. "Looks like you're makin' progress to me. Four guys have touched her since we've been standing here."

"They shook her hand," Qasim clarified.

"What about the one who kissed her cheek?"

"Ah, yeah." Qasim rubbed his jaw. "I forgot about him. We'll chat later," he said, joining in when the other man laughed.

"Proud of you, man." Robb clapped Qasim's shoulder.

"And you haven't even heard my news." Qasim let the suspense hang for a few quiet seconds. "I apologized to Lew for threatening him when he was going to ask Vectra out."

Robb's brows lifted in a clear sign of how impressed he was. "What brought that on?"

Qasim shrugged, watching Vectra as she moved around the room, charming her guests with little more than a brilliant smile or wink from her smoky-brown eyes.

He loved her.

"I don't want to be that kind of man," he told Robb. "She deserves better than that.'

Robb patted his old friend's back. "Like I said, I'm proud of you, man."

Qasim pushed Robb off and grinned. His eyes returned to Vectra talking with the featured artist near one of the gigantic canvases that decorated the gallery.

He loved her.

Robb patted his back, and Qasim realized he'd forgotten the man had even been there.

Robb groaned. "Like I said, a month."

"Can you come home with me?"

Vectra smiled, melting instantly into Qasim when he eased his arms about her waist later that evening.

She wanted nothing more.

Unfortunately, her conversations with Minka throughout the evening were all but crushing her romantic desires.

This was so not her business and yet Minka was practically begging her to intervene on her behalf. She'd do it. Of course she would, whether it was her business or not. She could see the other woman's fear. Minka never told her the specifics of Will Lloyd's comments to her about his possible impropriety with foundation funds, but her fear was all too easy to read.

"Hey." Qasim turned her in his arms.

Vectra focused her stare as though mentally snapping herself back into the situation. "I won't get done here till late," she explained.

"You think I mind?" His words were a gruff purr as he proceeded to drop kisses along her neck.

It occurred to Vectra that they were standing virtually in sight of everyone left in the gallery. The event had been a rousing success. Yancey Croachman had sold every canvas, with offers for more pieces and showings following her next appearance at Vectra's Gallery V–Miami in less than three weeks.

Just then, however, the success of the event wasn't Vectra's top thought. Instead, it was what Qasim's mouth was doing to her earlobe that had her full attention.

"Do you know where we're standing?" she asked softly.

"Hadn't thought about it," he murmured, obviously more focused on what his mouth was doing, as well.

"We're standing in the middle of the second-floor balcony." The area in question overlooked the first floor and was visible to everyone in the gallery.

Qasim's hand firmed on her hip, keeping her in place. "There a reason I need to know that?"

Vectra jerked in response. His free hand

was suddenly occupied by what it found inside the bodice of her dress. "I thought you'd want to know everyone can see us from here." Her words were a lazy drawl.

"So?" Her gasp drew his pitch-black stare to her face. "That a problem for you?"

"No, I just —"

"Just?"

"I said —"

"Said what?"

She slapped his shoulder. "Stop it."

"Stop what? This?" He resumed the deft feasting upon her earlobe.

"Sim . . . wait . . ."

He smiled, perfect teeth latching to her diamond-studded lobe. Eventually, he took pity. "What are you trying to tell me, V?"

Vectra took a second or three to steady her breathing. "I said I was all right with just sex, but if we keep this up, people will think we're in some kind of relationship."

"And that would be a bad thing?"

"No, I —"

"What? What are you saying?"

She stilled, dropping her stare to the banded collar of the white shirt beneath his dark suit jacket.

"Do you want to discuss this here?" he asked.

"Um, no. I — no." She collected herself,

remembering the business at hand. "We've got a little thing after the showing with the artist and her people. It's our usual wrap-up."

"Mmm-hmm." He sounded utterly disinterested and resumed his maddening nibble at her ear. "Come to me when you're done?"

"Sim." She paused to swallow down emotion. "We need to talk."

"We'll talk, too."

Exasperated, yet unable to pose the slightest argument over it, Vectra rested her forehead to Qasim's chest.

He propped her chin up with the curve of his fist. "You okay?"

"Things are spinning," she said on a breath. "I was okay with sex," she latched on in a bewildered tone.

His responding smile was adorable in its intensity. He'd set her completely off kilter and it thrilled him.

"I'm okay with sex, too, babe." He shook his head. "You've made it impossible for me to accept only that, though."

Great, she thought.

He wanted more and there she was about to overstep into matters that were none of her business. Not to mention the fact that she'd be putting the man who saved his life in a bad light. This wasn't going to be fun, but perhaps it was necessary and for more reasons than one.

Overstepping had once shown her the true colors of a man she thought she'd known all too well. Her conscience called her reasoning unfair. She knew it was without having to be told.

Forcing a smile, she smoothed the lapels of his jacket. The shirt beneath it called for no tie and settled her attention to the base of his throat for a time.

"I need to go home to the vineyard tonight." She met his gaze with hers. "Will you come there?"

Something changed in his eyes, and he lowered his head a fraction. "Understand that if I come there, I stay the night."

"Understood." She knew he'd probably not stay long past her accusing his old friend of being a thief.

Invading the rest of her personal space, Qasim brushed his mouth across the corner of hers. "I love you," he said.

He was gone before her shock over the admission took hold.

CHAPTER 15

Vectra was pleased to find the main house vacated when she returned from the showing well after midnight. Qasim had not arrived, so she used the time to change out of the gorgeous gown and into her standard lounge attire of sleep pants and a cotton halter tee.

Deciding that the impending conversation called for something more sobering than wine, she took time to prepare a pot of coffee with slices of banana cake to accompany it. While the coffee brewed, Vectra thought about Will Lloyd. Not surprisingly, though, her thoughts kept drifting to Qasim's parting words.

He loved her? Did he mean that, or was it just a flip tack-on he'd decided to use instead of goodbye? The pot beeped, and she smiled, going to see to the fresh brew.

She'd known Qasim long enough to know that the man didn't do flip. He'd left the gallery without waiting for her to reciprocate the confession, and she'd wanted to. She'd very much wanted to. But was she supposed to squeeze that in before or after they talked about Will?

The doorbell saved her from having to come up with an answer to that one.

Vectra left off preparing the coffee tray and sprinted toward the front of the house. She pulled open the door to a glowering Qasim.

"Does vineyard living mean you don't have to ask who's at the door?"

Taking no offense to the question, Vectra grabbed his jacket sleeve and pulled him inside. "It doesn't mean that, but *sometimes* it means you have the luxury of pretty good security." She pushed the door closed and gave a wave. "Come on in. I just made some coffee."

He caught the hem of her tee before she got too far. "It'll keep."

"We need to talk."

Qasim crowded her suddenly. Drawing her close, he tipped back her chin to deliberately probe her eyes with his. "I love you, Vectra, I meant that."

"How —" Her breath caught, yet she fought to speak through it. "How can you be sure? We haven't been seeing each other that long."

"We've known each other over two years. If you think I enjoyed being your friend because I was in business with your dad, you're very mistaken."

"You did stop enjoying it after a while," she pointed out.

Qasim acknowledged the fact with a smile. "I've never been any good at lying to myself. I said it so you'd know where I was coming from. You're it for me."

"Sim." His name was hushed on her lips, and she gave a start over the tears that suddenly blurred her eyes.

He grinned. "Is it *that* bad?"

Vectra gave a watery laugh. "It's not bad at all. But I'm no expert at this, and I'm terrified I'll mess it up. My last serious involvement didn't turn out so well, you know?"

Temper flared in his deep stare. "You had nothing to do with the way that turned out."

She smiled. "I had quite a bit to do with it, though. It takes two to make a relationship."

"Stop."

"No, Sim, I need you to understand that I played a part."

Instead of telling her to shut up, Qasim merely lifted her high. His hands provided a firm cradle for her bottom, and he punished her with a branding kiss.

At least, Vectra thought, it was a punishing kiss for even daring to take any part of the blame for the abuse she suffered. He was right. Hell, yes, he was right. She knew that, but it didn't diminish the fact that she was terrified of repeating mistakes that had led to some pretty nasty situations.

The branding kiss was hot, wet and deep. Vectra met it with her own manner of claiming, using the act to tell Qasim that she wanted all he had to give.

If only the little reminder warning would cease its shrill chiming inside her head. She didn't want to talk or do anything that didn't involve the two of them exclusively, but she'd put this off long enough.

"Um —" she tensed, working up just a hint of resistance "— we need to talk." Her voice wouldn't shed its moaning intensity.

"Not interested," he growled. With that, he carried her deeper into the house, taking the previous path he'd charted to her bedroom.

"Coffee . . ." she weakly offered, feeling his laughter vibrate from his chest through hers. In that moment, she couldn't resist laughing at herself. After all, she certainly hadn't dressed for serious conversation, had she?

"Not interested in coffee, either," he said.

Fevered kisses resumed, stopping only when Qasim broke stride to trap Vectra along one side of the stairway banisters. There, he released his hold on her bottom and moved it once again to the hem of her tee. He quickly jerked the garment over her head and left it on the stairs.

Qasim lost himself in the fullness of her breasts, which had been bare beneath the cotton top. Cupping both caramel globes, he eased his tongue between them and then circled his nose about her nipples until they marbled and strained for his attention.

Vectra squeezed his shoulders and attempted to steady herself against the banister. She slid her hands up, raking the silky whiskers shading his face. Upwards she traveled, until her fingers curled into the hair sleekly capping his head. She tried to direct him to take her into his mouth. Useless. He seemed content with tormenting her into oblivion with the scintillating glides his tongue made about her areola.

Qasim carried out the act while pulling Vectra from the banister to continue their ascent to the third level.

Vectra could sense the change in lighting

behind her closed lids as they ventured to the upper, dimmer floors. She reveled in Qasim's strength and sense of direction. His abilities allowed her to focus only on what he was doing to her body. She heard a door slam, and her eyes opened with a flutter of lashes to discover they were passing through the outer room of her bedroom suite.

Moments later, Vectra felt the semifirm cushioning of the mattress beneath her back. He took possession of one of her nipples, and her body became a sensual arc.

Qasim finally obliged her. Sucking as though he were famished, he manipulated one nipple with his tongue and teeth while he exquisitely tortured the other beneath his thumb.

Vectra cursed the snug sleep pants still hugging her lower half. Her hips commenced a wicked sway beneath his. She gasped, wrecked by the triple sensations stemming from his mouth, fingers and the deliciously ridged arousal pressed against her.

Qasim muttered something incomprehensible. Her nudges against his erection were driving him out of his mind. Well . . . more out of his mind than he'd already been driven by her, eager and beautiful beneath him.

Blindly, he groped for the barrier still separating her from his touch. The pants she wore proved no match for the insistence of his fingers once they'd curled into the material and wrenched it free of her body.

"Dammit, Sim!" she gasped when the material ripped. "They were my favorite."

"I'll make it up," he soothed.

It was no use. She was newly dismayed when her achy, glistening nipples were suddenly abandoned. Vectra lashed out to skim his shoulder with a fist, but she only hit air. Opening her eyes, she saw that he'd sat up to remove his shirt.

Vectra was quite pleased by the opportunity to watch the material slowly peel away to reveal the muscle-packed licorice plane of his chest. Her nipples ached with renewed awareness, yearning to feel the sleek wall against her.

Qasim's intentions ran along a different course, however. Once he'd discarded the shirt, he spread her thighs to accommodate his wide frame. Vectra's heart jumped into her throat, beating in sync with the slow thrum of her need. Eagerly, she anticipated his next move.

Qasim set his thumb against her clit. His dark eyes narrowed as he watched Vectra's reactions. She bit down on her bottom lip and rolled her hips when he used his other thumb to circle a nipple in slow sweeps.

The move sent sparks of erotic radiation throughout her sex-hungry body. Her hips bucked right off the bed when Qasim claimed the heart of her in one potent tongue thrust. He gripped her hips, steadying her without ever breaking his oral claim on her core. Vectra felt him drop several possessive taps to her thigh — a warning to stay put.

Sensually vexed, she spread her hands up and outward over the bed, sheltering them beneath the hoard of pillows near the top. Slowly, she rocked her hips in time to the thrusts and rotations of his tongue.

Qasim's hunger had reached insatiable heights. His arousal was a painful ache below his waist, made more so due to the fact that it was still confined behind his trousers.

Amidst her pleasure haze, Vectra angled her foot beneath Sim's waist to test the extent of his need. She smiled brightly when he shuddered in response.

Vectra's naughty move was the final straw for Qasim. He pushed up once more, this time to relieve himself of his pants, shoes, socks and boxers. He snagged several condom packets from his trousers before tossing the garment free of the bed.

Power and passion surged through Vectra like some enhanced version of adrenaline. Easily, she pushed Qasim to his back and took possession of the condoms. With a drugging touch, she applied their protection while dragging her tongue from Qasim's collarbone, down his sternum, across the devastating array of abdominal muscles and finally teasing his navel. She straddled his body, her back to him, and eased the casing over his shaft, which was as impressive in length as it was in girth.

Her lips parted on a soft sigh as she anticipated the enticing endowment inside her. Milliseconds after setting the condom in place, she felt her hips seized in a viselike hold. Qasim lifted and settled her with exquisite mastery, her back facing him, and proceeded to stretch her with his throbbing solidness.

Vectra threw back her head to hiss out Qasim's name, the sound leaving her throat on a husky groan. Her breathing came in broken hiccups as he conducted her body to his satisfaction. He lifted and rotated her hips, smothered in his big hands. He released her to smooth his palms over her upper thighs and back.

Vectra's head sloped forward. She rode

him enthusiastically in the reverse-cowgirl position, and the room grew colored by the mingled sounds of their throaty moans. The faint slapping of skin as their bodies rhythmically connected and reconnected merely enhanced their passionate desperation.

Qasim was sensitive enough to know Vectra was moments from coming apart on him. He wasn't ready for that, but, damn, if she didn't feel too good to tear away from.

The systematic clench and release of her sexual muscles tossed him over wave after seductive wave. Qasim's deep voice was faint as he grunted out her name each time she squeezed and milked him. He spilled his seed into the condom, his body shaking as he both cursed and celebrated his loss of control.

Vectra slumped forward, surrendering to her own shattering release. Once depleted, she fell back against Qasim. She took her time catching her breath and enjoying the soothing sensation of her back sealed flat against his chest. She flinched a little when his palm smoothed down her front, not stopping until he'd covered her mound. They were still intimately connected, and she felt her sex react as though it had its own agenda. Her sensitive muscles clutched at his organ. Semierect, it still felt amazing inside her.

Vectra bucked gently against his hand when he pinched her clit between his thumb and forefinger. He then soothed the spot beneath his middle finger, which quickly labored her breathing.

Qasim steadied her rolling hips beneath one hand, his erection firming and lengthening to breathtaking depth inside her for another exquisite round.

Vectra woke the next morning flat on her back and twisted in a tangle of covers. She was there alone. Relief and agitation both stirred. Relief because she needed a little more time to recover from last night's escapades. Qasim Wilder could retire from finance and bottle his stamina instead. She had a feeling his income wouldn't suffer in the least.

Then there was her case of mild agitation. She hadn't come close to getting into what they were really supposed to be doing the night before — discussing *his* business.

Vectra massaged her eyes and lay there, debating on whether to leave the bed or roll over into a more comfortable position, when she heard soft male laughter followed by a distinct feminine twitter. Frowning, Vectra pushed herself up to rest her weight on her elbows. She waited for the sound to repeat. It did, and it had her leaving the bed to investigate.

The sight meeting her eyes when she pulled open the door had her fascinated. Qasim was in the outer room leaning against the fireplace mantel and looking quite at home in his trousers and partially buttoned shirt. His bare feet and the mug he held lent to the "at home" look.

What held her stunned, though, was the sight of Charlotte seated on one of the chaise longues. The woman was in a fit of giggles over whatever had just come out of Qasim's mouth. Vectra gave an awkward wave when they noticed her standing in the doorway, clothed in the sheet she'd tied in a sarong about her body.

Laughter curving to a sly smile, Charlotte left the lounge chair and gave Vectra a teasing once-over.

"Good morning." Charlotte's greeting was quiet and meaningful as she strode from the room.

"Guess the cat's out of the bag," Qasim said once he'd drained the contents of his mug.

She blurted the first question that came to mind. "Why'd you spend the night?"

He didn't look pleased. "You know why. I told you why."

Vectra trudged out into the room. "We need to talk."

"Love to —" his eyes raked her body appreciatively "— but I need to get going." He appeared slightly repentant. "I didn't mean to spill the beans to Charlotte, but I didn't want to leave before you woke up."

Vectra surveyed her attire, knowing it was far from appropriate, but she could waste no more time. He needed to hear what she had to say before he left for the office.

Qasim placed his mug to the mantel. Closing the distance between him and Vectra, he scooped her up, sheets and all.

"Sim . . ." She sighed in response to the slow, thorough kiss he treated her to.

"I'll be back," he murmured against her mouth and then pulled back just a tad to observe her attire. "Could I request *this* outfit?"

She clutched his shirt. "Sim, please? I really need to talk to you."

Qasim dropped a quick, pacifying kiss to the corner of her mouth. He let her ease down the length of him until her feet reached the floor. "When I get back, okay? I already put in my dinner request with the cook staff." He winked, hoping the gesture masked his worry and reluctance to hear her tell him that she wasn't ready or able to commit to the relationship he very much wanted to share with her.

Vectra watched him return to the bedroom, where he hunted down his socks and shoes.

"I need to talk to you about Will," she said, watching as he tied his second loafer. "Will Lloyd," she unnecessarily clarified, swallowing when he stilled and shifted his black gaze to her.

"What about Will Lloyd?"

His question sounded soft, stilted. Vectra rubbed at her eyes in an attempt to stop their rapid blinking. When she looked up again, he was right before her.

"What did he say to you?"

Qasim had apologized to Will for ordering him not to speak or even look at Vectra. He knew, though, that there was someplace deep and dark inside him where the apology hadn't quite rung true. "What'd he say, Vectra?"

"Nothing —"

"Vectra," he snarled.

She winced, but wasn't about to lose her nerve when she'd already said so much. Besides, it was too important to back down from.

"He didn't say anything to me. It was Minka."

Somehow Qasim's scowl increased in menacing potency. His reaction was Vectra's only hint that he'd heard what she'd said.

"She wouldn't tell me what he said to her specifically, but she's got reason to believe Will's been . . . helping himself to foundation money. She says she can prove it. Will suspects she knows. I–I don't know what he's threatening to do if she said anything to you so . . ." She stretched her lips in an awkward smile and shrugged. "She came to me."

Qasim shook his head in a way that signified he'd heard enough. He turned, buttoning his shirt while stalking the room for keys, which had slipped from his trouser pockets the night before. Locating them, he left the room without another word to Vectra.

CHAPTER 16

"Sim? Man, you wanted to see me?"

Qasim looked up from the folder he'd been studying and tilted his head back slightly to acknowledge Will Lloyd's greeting.

"Have a seat," he called.

"Sorry I'm late." Will made his way to the lounge area of Qasim's office. "Didn't realize running a charity required so much number crunching. It's a good thing I'm a math freak." He grinned. "But that's probably why it's so easy for me to lose track of time when I get goin' with something."

"Well, your math and social skills are what got you this job, you know?"

Will's grin took on a devilish tint. "Thought I got the job because of my lifesaving act of valor on a sandbank a few years back?"

Grinning as well, Qasim stood as Will took a seat in one of the leather box-style chairs that flanked a matching sofa. "It didn't get you the job, but it's the reason I've kept you around as long as I have."

Will's easy expression betrayed signs of strain at the edges. He served up no rebuttal, however.

Qasim passed the chair his old friend was occupying. Along the way, he dropped the folder he'd been studying into Will's lap. "You don't really have to read that," he said. "My guess is you're pretty familiar with it, anyway. It's more for me so I can keep it all together, especially when there's so much of it and it's been going on for so long."

Will managed a curious laugh and checked the contents of the folder. Qasim watched the expressions change on the other man's face and smirked.

"You notice the docs in that folder date back almost two years — about ten months after you came on board as the foundation's business director."

The folder tumbled from Will's hands.

"Couldn't you have at least given me a year, man? Just one year before confirming what I suspected about you from the first day we met?" Qasim asked, walking back to his desk. "I actually doubted myself." He tapped his palm to the front of the vest he wore over a dark shirt. "It's not every day I doubt myself, but, well . . . you *did* save my life and all."

"Sim —"

"I'm real big on oversight committees, Will. They do more than point out mistakes. They keep people honest . . . most of the time."

Qasim strode to the front of his desk. "You were good. The folks on that committee are no slouches, but you managed to keep them three steps behind. I had no reason to doubt you." He perched on a corner of the sectional desk. "I mean, you *did* save my life and all."

Qasim's repetition of the fact made Will flinch as though the words were a slap.

"I wouldn't buy it when they came to me with their suspicions," Sim continued. "I got pretty upset. It wasn't a good scene. I told 'em to leave it alone, but oversight committees . . ." He winced. "They don't always listen. As you can see —" he nodded toward the pages scattered at Will's feet "— the docs in that folder look like duplicates, and they are — invoices of charges connected to foundation events. Only one shows the charge actually quoted by the vendors minus the little service fee you quoted to us. They got us to take another look at those exorbitant rates quoted by our usual hotels. Turns out they didn't go up nearly as much as we first thought — or were told."

Will moved to the edge of his chair. "Sim —"

"Save it. They asked me to fire you not long after I hired you, but I let you stay because I wanted you in jail and suffering in all those ways they love to make you suffer there." Qasim left the desk and began to prowl the far side of the office.

"I knew your ego would get the better of you and we'd be on our way to having you good and tight once you had that signing doc, but then Minka figured your act. And then you had the nerve to threaten her."

"I never —"

"And I couldn't have you stick around after that." Qasim scratched the whiskers shading his jaw. "Your office is being cleaned out. Everything will be stacked up nice and neat by the time your lawyer gets you released."

"Released!" Will bolted from the chair, sputtering the word.

"Don't worry. You won't be in there nearly as long as you deserve."

"Sim —"

"Get out of my sight."

A hard knock followed the order. Two

uniformed guards looked into the office.

"You done, sir?" one of the men queried.

Qasim threw up a hand. "Completely. Thanks, guys."

Will jerked off the hold when he was secured. Qasim raised a hand to stay the guards.

"You owe me, Sim!"

"What? A job wasn't good enough?"

"For what I did? No way!"

Qasim smirked. "So why didn't you just ask me for money instead of taking money from those kids? I'd have given it to you."

"Self-righteous idiot." Will sneered. "You probably wanted to crap bricks when I saved your life. A nobody like me."

"We were all nobodies." Qasim gave a mystified shrug. "Why'd you track me down? Was it really the hard-luck story you gave me two years back, or did you just want to bring me down a few?"

Will remained belligerent. "There was enough in those expense accounts alone. I never took a dime away from the special accounts for your brats."

"And that makes it all right?"

Will balled his fists, punching out at the air. "Damn that wench, Minka!"

"You're a dead man if you go near her." Qasim's cool veneer turned noticeably rigid.

Will feigned surprise. "Should I tell my lawyer I've just been threatened?"

"You've been guaranteed. Guys?" Qasim called to his guards. "Do I stand by my guarantees?"

"Absolutely, sir," the men chimed in enthusiastic smugness.

One of the guards opened the office door. The other waved a hand before Will.

"Sir?" the man prodded.

Qasim maintained his barely restrained anger until the guards had escorted Will from the office. Alone, Qasim spent long moments inhaling and working tight knots of frustration from his neck and shoulders. He tried to ease Will's betrayal to the back of his mind, but only found his temper stirring more as a result. Finally, he realized only one thing — one woman — had the power to settle whatever riled him.

If Oscar Bauer thought it strange that his daughter called suddenly to request information on his potential retirement digs along the Italian coast, he made no indication of it.

Vectra was glad since she didn't really know what to make of it herself. The word "coward" came to mind, but she didn't begrudge it. Leaving for Lake Misurina,

Italy, may have been a touch much, but her father had asked her to make the trip, hadn't he?

Of course, Vectra knew that wasn't why she suddenly insisted on snagging a flight and leaving the house two hours after Qasim's heated departure. No doubt he'd been enraged, she thought, recalling the livid glint in his midnight gaze when he'd stormed out. A flurry of vile curses had streamed after him.

Leaving the way she had hadn't been necessary, but she'd panicked. Old memories hastened her departure in spite of the fact that a trip was already in her immediate future. After Italy, she'd be headed to Miami, where she'd oversee the final preparations for Yancey Croachman's next showing. There wouldn't be much to handle, she knew. Once the artist's vision for the first show was underway, the Miami staff would take its cues from the event. The follow-up show wouldn't require nearly as much extensive planning.

So why was she adding another leg to her trip?

Vectra wouldn't allow herself to mull over the answer for long.

Lake Misurina was a dream. Vectra had

decided her father had made an excellent choice within minutes of her arrival less than twenty-four hours earlier. The lake, site of previous Olympic speed skating events, was known for its crisp, clean air that beckoned asthma sufferers and athletes alike.

Oscar Bauer's intended digs were just as beckoning. The villa overlooked the lake and the Tre Cime di Lavaredo in the distance. From the master bedroom terrace, Vectra inhaled, accepting the air's rejuvenating effects while soaking in the glory of the mountains.

As beautiful as it all was, though, she only wanted to be back in her bed waiting for Qasim's return.

Boy, you really screwed this one up, didn't you, Vec?

She really had, but the knowledge didn't erase the fact that too much of her past was still hanging around.

So, now what?

She turned her back on the view, leaning along the rail as she bit at her thumbnail. She thought — hoped — she was beyond all that, beyond second-guessing or examining everything she did for signs that it was all prompted by her past.

It all came down to disclosure, full

disclosure. She'd never been able to do that, not with her family, not with anyone. She hadn't wanted to ever be reminded of how weak she'd been during that entire mess with Keith Freedman.

Was it fair to ask Qasim to wait around until she was ready to share? And what if she was never ready to share it? What a mess . . . And *she* was the one who had created it. If only she had kept quiet about her more-than-friends desires for Qasim.

Then, she never would've known she still had the ability to love someone. Discovering that had made it all so worth it. Even so, she needed to come clean with Qasim. Of course, she was terrified to bare her soul that way, but he deserved to know all there was. That, after all, was what it meant to love.

She dug her phone out from the back pocket of her jeans and sent her father a text to bestow quick blessings upon his oasis of choice. Then, she logged into the airline website to confirm details for her return flight to the States. First Miami and then back to San Francisco. She could only pray she'd use the time away to figure out what to say to Qasim when she saw him.

"Sim?" Minka rushed into the office, looking flustered and confused. "What's going on? I just heard they cleaned out Will's office and he was taken out by security."

"Sit down, Mink." Qasim waited for her to settle into one of the chairs in his office's gaming area. "Why didn't you come to me about this?"

Minka bowed her head and gave it a weary shake. "So that's why you insisted I take the day off." She smiled sadly and then looked up at him. "I didn't think you'd believe me."

"Minka —"

"No, Sim." She stood. "I've heard all the stories about how you behaved when the oversight committee tried to tell you about Will before." She tousled her hair while she paced the room.

"I'd already showed him up by suggesting we use Vectra's place for the foundation event. Coming to you with more . . . I'd have looked pretty petty, wouldn't you say? Besides, I didn't have anything concrete until he left those invoices and I was able to use them for comparison."

"I started keeping an eye on Will after the committee shared their suspicions." Qasim lifted his heavy brows in a quick up-and-down move when Minka's face betrayed her surprise.

"I know they had merit," he went on. "I

wanted him gone, too, and not just fired but behind bars and doing *hard* time." Qasim commenced to stalking the opposite side of the room. "I didn't want him working for another committee, organization, corporation — nothing. That's why I kept on kept feeding that ego of his. I know you stalled on giving him that signing form."

Again, Minka appeared stunned. "Why didn't you say anything to me?"

Qasim had the decency to appear sheepish. "My mind's been on other things lately, and Will's antics weren't as important to me as they should've been."

"I understand." Minka smiled before glancing at the office door. "You think that's the last we'll see of him?"

"Doubtful." Qasim massaged his neck behind the open collar of his shirt. "Given that he doesn't think he's done anything wrong."

"So what now?"

"Now —" Qasim retrieved his suit coat from the back of a chair "— I'm taking the rest of the week off. Direct my calls — legal and otherwise — to Price." He referred to Price Bonderson, Wilder's director of legal affairs.

"No problem. Have fun," Minka bade.

Qasim stopped before the woman and

gave her a level stare. "Never keep anything like this from me again, all right?"

Minka seemed relieved. "All right. I only hope nothing like this ever happens again."

"Nothing that raises your suspicion is ever too petty for you to come to me with. It's what I depend on you for."

"Hmph." Minka shook her head. "That's what Vectra tried to tell me."

"She was right." Qasim thought of the woman he loved.

"So is that where — or *who* — you're headed off to see?"

"I think I scared her a little the way I tore out of her house the other day," he admitted.

Minka sighed. "Qasim, I really am sorry about Will. He was your friend, after all."

"It was a friendship born out of gratitude, not mutual interest, and one I'm not sad to see the end of." Qasim reached out, gave Minka a tiny shake.

"Never hide anything like this again, Mink."

She gave a solemn shake of her head. "I won't."

CHAPTER 17

Miami Beach, Florida

Vectra didn't usually take the time to enjoy all that the city had to offer. Seeing as how the staff at Gallery V–Miami had things well in hand for Yancey Croachman's upcoming show, there wasn't much that required her constant presence there.

The trip itself had been unnecessary, as she'd figured, but that was another story. She had been gone almost four days and Qasim hadn't tried to contact her since. She'd gotten consistent with forcing herself to change her train of thought when she silently reminded herself of the fact that it was what she'd wanted. Furthermore, she contented herself that she must have been dead-on with Qasim's attitude about prying into his business.

Just as well, she thought, closing her eyes and trying to allow the serenity and shade of the dock to relax her.

She'd decided on a condo instead of one of the palatial beachfront homes that epitomized South Beach living. On a smaller scale, the condo was a stunning place in its own right. The dwelling was awash in sun and splashes of color from the floor-to-ceiling windows. The turquoise waters of an infinity pool spanned almost half the condo's expansive brick deck.

Vibrantly textured furnishings complemented the wall canvases and throw pillows. They filled the open lower level and more private rooms on the second floor.

Vectra enjoyed her solitude even as she criticized her handling of the situation.

"You could've done this same thing in California, you know?"

She jerked into an upright stance on the lounge so fast that the chair's legs scraped the brick deck.

"Sim? How . . . ?"

Qasim didn't need her to finish. "You mean, how did I track you down here based on the note you left? Well, I didn't since you didn't leave me one."

"Sim —"

"So once I got past the shock of you doing something so stupid and impolite, I thanked Charlotte for sharing what little details she had about your sudden travel

251

plans." He lifted his hands slightly before letting them fall back to his sides. "Here I am."

With slow, grounding breaths, Vectra left the lounge once she felt up to standing. She noticed the downward trail Qasim's eyes took when he appraised the lavender bikini she had pranced around in for the better part of the day.

She'd decided against walking inside for a cover-up and leaned along the back of the deck sofa. She hoped the stance might de-emphasize her current state of dress.

"I knew you'd be busy after we talked . . . about Will."

"Right . . ." His nod was deliberately slow. "So naturally you had to leave the country?"

"Sim . . ."

"Why'd you go, *really*?"

"Qasim, I don't like having to step in on matters related to your business."

"Vectra —"

She resisted the urge to wince when he growled her name. "I swear it's true. Those kinds of deeds haven't done me any favors in the past."

"What the hell does that mean?" Qasim didn't realize how angry he was until he was standing within touching distance of her.

After leaving Carro, where the

housekeeper, Charlotte Sweeney, had to
him of Vectra's sudden and unexpected
departure, he'd set out to find her. Accord-
ing to Charlotte, Vectra had skedaddled
little more than an hour following his own
heated exit. He'd expected that she may
have been unsettled by his reaction to what
she told him about Will, but enough to leave
town? Hell, the country? He guessed so.

"How'd you find me?" she asked.

If Qasim noticed that she'd sidestepped
his question, he didn't mention it. "Charlotte said something about you checking out
the Miami gallery. I checked with the gallery back home, told them I might want to
see the one here, too, maybe organize a
thing, considering how well it all went during the tasting event . . ." He shrugged.
"They were all too happy to help — even
called the gallery out here and they went
the extra mile to tell me you were working
—" he cut off to indulge in another scandal-
ous rake of her body "— from home today,
but they made sure to square things with
the office downstairs. They granted me access when I arrived." He studied the life
lines in his palms as though the action
calmed him.

"This was all after your father called to
tell me you were in Italy and asked why

sn't I there with you when he told you to
take me."

Vectra lowered herself into deck sofa. "You
were busy . . ."

"You said that already."

"Sim . . ."

"I'm listening."

"He saved your life."

"You're my life."

Her breath caught, and she sat there,
blinking up at him in wonder.

Qasim roared a sharp, ill-humored laugh.
"Did you think I was 'just playing' when I
told you I loved you? What the hell do you
think that means?"

"Not always what you think!" She cursed
quietly over the slip and left the chair, holding her hands to her mouth as she paced
the deck.

Qasim strode over and sank into the space
Vectra had vacated. He leaned forward,
bracing his elbows to the jeans shorts where
they covered his knees.

"Everyone I consider a friend knows their
parents — both of them," he said. "Do you
know how rare that is in the world I come
from? Most folks at least know their mother.
I don't know either of my parents." He
studied his palms again.

"The only thing my mother did for me

was to give me a name before she left me at the hospital. I fought my way through foster care and group homes knowing I only had to make it to eighteen." He shrugged and turned his striking gaze out across the deck.

"It made me fight harder. That kind of living — that kind of childhood — screws with your trust, your security, Vectra. In my world, if you weren't possessive of your stuff, if you didn't stake your claim, it got taken from you and then . . . the rage sets in. I guess it set in for me at an early age, and I . . ."

He forced a smile.

"When I was free, able to make my own decisions, so far as the law was concerned, I craved going to the army believing it'd be the only place I'd fit. It was the only place where the rage was encouraged. I found that it was . . . necessary to an extent, but what was truly encouraged was the ability to mold it, to control it.

"I had to learn that the hard way. Once I did, that's when I was free. In Will's defense, he never tells the full story of how he came to save my life — makes me look like a victim instead of somebody who was asking for it. He saved me from a guy who deserved to take me out. He was a prisoner I leaned on pretty hard. The guy spit in my face, and

I tried to beat him to death. I was stupid."
He shook his head again, the smile appearing more genuine.

"Stupid kid . . . I had attitude for days and a thing about respect — respect *I* was owed of course. It took four guys from my platoon to pull me off. Will was one of 'em.

"When he tackled me, the prisoner took his gun. Everybody froze but Will. He reacted. I shed a lot of my attitude that day. When he came to me down on his luck, I thought it was the least I could do . . ."

Qasim stood suddenly, looking to Vectra, who was then clutching the cushions along the back of her lounge chair for support.

"That's all of it, V. The part of me I don't share with anyone. Who I was isn't who I am. It may've played a role in the shaping, but it doesn't define me. Those dark areas crop up from time to time, but that's life, and I fight their hold however I can. No way am I going back to what I was. The same is true for you."

He advanced. "You have to believe that. You have to decide how long you're gonna let it keep coming back to bite you."

Qasim closed the distance remaining between them. Tugging her hand from the cushion, he kissed the back of it then

brushed a lingering one to her cheek.
"I love you," he said and was gone.

CHAPTER 18

Vectra stayed in Miami to be available for Yancey Croachman's follow-up gallery appearance. She hadn't planned on it until she'd received word that the Wilder Warriors Foundation event would be held in the city as opposed to her vineyard.

It was a smart move. The event had been pushed up to offset the drama with Will Lloyd. The man's dismissal from his post and the details of that dismissal had already made the rounds through Wilder. The foundation's planning committee, led once again by Minka Gerald, had decided to push up the annual fund-raiser before those details leaked over into public knowledge.

Though disappointed by the change in plan, Vectra knew it was a better move and had saved her household from being turned upside down. Still, the place had been abuzz with excitement regarding the gathering. Most, if not all, Carro employees had known or knew of someone who'd gone to school on a Wilder Foundation scholarship.

Vectra wouldn't let herself believe that the final decision was in any way personal or that Qasim would hold a grudge. He'd said that he loved her, and she believed him. She felt the same. He'd bared his soul, and she . . . hadn't done the same. But she didn't need to, did she? Qasim was right. *This* was going to keep coming back to bite her unless she fought it and kept fighting. He had been so forthcoming with her. She had to verbalize her fears and verbalize them to the man she loved.

The Hembry Downtown had been the site of the Wilder Warriors Foundation events in years past. The hotel enveloped its visitors with a '20s vibe. The architecture was understated elegance speaking to the charm of the era.

The Hembry was a testament to the jazz culture and speakeasy flavor of the time. It was the perfect setting for the event taking place that evening. The planned costume ball wasn't scheduled until the following night, but Vectra figured she'd go on and get decked out in the spirit of things. She wore a dazzling silver fringe hem dress that adored her every curve just as the matching vintage-inspired T-strap pumps accentuated the stunning length of her legs. Her pixie cut was the perfect style for the evening and went well with the '20s-fashion cloche hat.

May as well go all out, she thought. She had no idea how the evening might turn out. She might not be back to enjoy more of the extravaganza. Vectra closed her eyes, commanding herself not to think the worst. She tethered her thoughts and steadied her steps with the reminder that Qasim Wilder loved her.

A waiter, dressed in a classic tux befitting the time period, stopped to offer champagne. Vectra accepted a flute of the bubbly beverage without hesitation. She sipped, smiling faintly at the hint of fruit she detected in the otherwise dry blend. Covertly, she surveyed the crowd, eager to find Qasim and not quite sure what she'd say or do when she did.

The matter was offset for a while, at least, when she spotted Minka. The woman was making her way to one of the chesterfield-style sofas that dotted an enormous gold-and-cream checkerboard lobby where the opening party was being held.

"Minka!" Vectra made her way over to the woman, watching as she reconsidered taking a spot on the antique furnishing.

Minka's trademark sunny smile flashed. "Vectra!" She pulled her close for a hug. "So glad you could come!"

"Yeah, well . . ." Vectra scanned the lovely, glamorous room. "I wanted to see what the competition has that I didn't."

"Sorry about the change." Minka's apology mirrored her expression of regret. "We really did feel bad about putting such an event on you in the first place." Minka studied the sumptuous room, as well. "We've been thinking about a Gatsby-type weekend event for a long time, though. Given the Hembry's recent renovations to maintain their vintage style . . . we thought it'd be the perfect locale." Minka winced. "Then we got their pricing sheet and we weren't so sure."

"Ahh . . ." Vectra offered a mock toast with her glass. "Pricing with a little extra tacked on by Will Lloyd."

"Hmph," Minka said, smirking. "He made it sound like the Hembry's recent maintenance work was to blame."

"And now, thanks to you —" Vectra raised a hand toward the chandelier's illuminated ceiling "— here we are."

"I didn't want to get here like this." Minka sighed. "Feels like I had to crawl through a lake of mud in Pettysville, USA."

"Understood!" Vectra laughed, her eyes still sparkling well after the laughter quieted. "Sometimes we have to spend a little time in the dirt to get to the happy places in life."

Minka's expression brightened. "I like your optimism."

Vectra shrugged. "A good friend told me that dark areas crop up from time to time, but that's life."

The corners of Minka's mouth tilted down, proving that she was impressed. "Your friend sounds like a pretty smart person."

Vectra was about to respond. Instead, she blinked past Minka's shoulder. "He has his moments," she said.

Minka followed the path of Vectra's gaze and smiled up at her boss. "Hey, Sim — oh! Look who's here . . ." She acted as though she'd spotted someone across the crowded room. "I should go and say hi. Vectra, it was great to see you." She squeezed Sim's arm on the way past. "Don't forget I booked you a suite here for the weekend."

"Was that a hint?" Qasim grinned at Vectra once Minka had rushed off.

"I love you," she blurted, blinking uncontrollably while expelling the breath she didn't realize she was holding.

"I'm sorry. I–I should've said that a long

time ago — a long time before you told me."
She sipped down more champagne. "It was
why I really came to see you that day about
Robb's party. I — you cut me off, and I . . .
I didn't know why." She set the nearly
empty glass on a white lacquer end table
and stepped closer to Qasim.

"Losing your friendship that way when I
had all this —" she curved her hands toward
her chest as if to emphasize the emotion
crushing her from the inside "— I had —
have — all these feelings for you and
nowhere to put them. What I'm feeling isn't
for anyone else but you."

She inhaled deeply and expelled the
breath, needing the release following the
confession she'd kept to herself for far too
long.

Qasim schooled both his surprise and approval. He kept his smile soft, not wanting
to do anything to discourage her from telling him what she needed to.

Vectra looked miserable. "I'm sorry,
Qasim. I–I shouldn't have left town the way
I did, but I panicked and —"

He silenced her. Gently, he tugged one of
the fringed cap sleeves of her dress. He
pulled her close, her curves fitting perfectly
against his solid frame. His mouth crushed
hers, his tongue thrusting deep, exploring at

length before entwining with hers.

Desperately, Vectra caught the lapels of his three-quarter-length pinstriped jacket and fully participated in their kissing battle. She moaned, raking her nails across the whiskers darkening his jaw. Flames began to lick her with the same potency that Qasim's mouth branded her with. Someone passed and patted his back.

"The place has lots of rooms, man."

The couple broke their kiss, soft laughter humming between them.

"I've had enough of the hints," Qasim said close to her ear.

"Well, you can't leave." Vectra eased back as much as he'd allow, looking horrified.

"Why not?"

"Sim." She watched him, trying to determine whether he was teasing her. "This is *your* event. Your charity. Do you make a habit of leaving before these things get started?"

He shrugged. "Never had a reason to leave before."

She laughed. "Don't even try it. I read the society rags, same as everybody else. I've seen some of the candy on your arm. Sometimes there's candy on both of your arms."

"You're right." He flexed said arms around

264

her. "But this is the candy I'm in love with." He nuzzled her ear.

"Sim . . ." she murmured, wanting nothing more than for them to take their leave of the party. There was more she needed to say to him, after all, but there was time, she decided. Warmth flooded her body as the truth of the statement hit home.

"Have you even spoken to everyone yet?"

"No." He shrugged. "I rarely do since this thing will go on all weekend. Anyone I miss tonight, I'll see before it's all over."

Vectra gave the man she loved a chastising look. "And that doesn't make you feel guilty?"

"It doesn't."

She shook her head. "Well, it'd make *me* feel guilty if you left because of me. Now —" she managed to ease out of his hold, then turned the tables and eased a hand through the crook of his arm "— let me show you the art of the mingle-and-greet."

They ventured into the crowd, stopping by guests where they'd already collected in small clusters to chat. Vectra and Qasim spoke heartily yet briefly, not long enough to shift the topics of the conversations already in progress. It took about forty-five minutes for them to make their way around the grand room.

"You're a master at this," Qasim said once they stood waiting for the elevator that would whisk them up to his suite.

Vectra made a pretense of brushing her shoulders. "Why do you think I'm always on Dad's or Oliver's arm? They're always trying to make discreet exits." She slanted him a saucy wink.

"If you're attending an event that you need to dip out of early and it's *your* event, the mingle-and-greet lets you make your way around the room briefly speaking — *briefly* because the guests are already in conversations of their own.

"It works well with loners, too — they've been drawn into a conversation, however brief, but they don't feel quite as on edge afterwards, especially since they've been noticed by the guest of honor."

"Ingenious," Qasim said once Vectra had thoroughly explained her mingling technique.

"That last one I learned through experience. I was once very shy."

"Stop." He made a show of being stunned.

Vectra hit his arm in retaliation. "Being noticed at a party when I'm trying to go *un*noticed always took the pressure off."

Qasim couldn't imagine the woman seriously believed she could go unnoticed. "I'm afraid your dad and brother are going to have to do without you on their arms so much," he told her instead.

Vectra smiled. "Why?"

"A skill like yours is a hot commodity," he explained just as the elevator dinged its arrival. "I plan to have you on my arm every chance I get for the foreseeable future."

Qasim winked, waving to urge her procession into the car, and, thankfully, the elevator's ascent was brief.

Qasim didn't move away from the door once it had closed behind him and Vectra in his suite. Instead, he leaned back against the heavy pine door and kept Vectra close, her back to his chest. His mouth skimmed her shoulder and nape as his hands travelled her hips to toy with the fringe hem of her dress.

Vectra luxuriated in the sensation his fingertips radiated into her skin. They danced along the tops of her thighs, venturing toward the inner domain that part of her anatomy wanted him to find.

She put her hands to his with plans to still his pursuit. Instead, she traveled along with his touch as it honed in closer to her sex, which puckered against the cottony middle of her panties. She felt one of his hands suddenly curve in to hook around her inner thigh, keeping it spread away from its twin. She let her head rest back against his chest and gave in.

It couldn't hurt to indulge in just a few seconds of the delicious caress, she decided.

His middle finger stroked up and down the crotch of her panties while his thumb launched a second erotic assault on her clit. The circular caresses across the hub of sensation forced a litany of moans and gasps from her throat.

Vectra was boneless, a limp shell energized by the pure sensation that only enabled her to moan and writhe as she relied on Qasim's support to hold her up. Her moans gained volume, and then she was hiccupping Qasim's name when his finger delved beneath the barrier between it and her core. Her entire body tensed as her satiny walls clenched and trapped his finger.

"We have to talk," she sobbed. "Sim." She moaned when he responded by adding another thick finger to his wicked claiming of her body.

"Sim —"

"It can wait." He tongued her ear.

Vectra was drained of her pleas, accepting that he held no interest in them. Neither did she. She surrendered to the thrilling two-finger thrust that stirred her into a frenzy. Her hips rolled and bucked. She sought to embrace the sensations that collided through her quivering form, a result of his devilish handling of her sex. In minutes, it seemed, she was coming apart in his arms. A fierce orgasm ricocheted through her.

Qasim gave her less than a minute to recover from her release. Then, he scooped her high, carrying her through the graceful, classically furnished suite to the bedroom in the back. He sat down to the foot of the bed, still carrying her. His hands still cupped her bottom.

Vectra straddled his lap and went to work on the custom-made jacket and shirt he wore. She pulled the garments from his wide back and shoulders. Qasim found his way under her dress, hooking his thumbs inside the crotch of her panties and using them to simultaneously stimulate the silken slit of her femininity.

Vectra bit down on her lip, eager to be ushered into a second climax. Qasim had other ideas, choosing instead to get her out of her dress and under things.

"Cooperate or I'll tear it off your back," he murmured in a teasing whisper, smiling when she dutifully raised her arms.

He gave no such instruction regarding her

269

panties. Those, he ripped away with one effective tug to the crotch. Still, he refused to give her what she wanted. Fixated on her breasts bouncing before his face, he cupped the caramel-hued orbs. While rolling one nipple between thumb and forefinger, he gave the other the benefit of an intense suck. Her hiccupping gasp near his ear was as much a stimulant as the feel of her nipple marbling on his tongue.

She urged him on with whispered words while pushing more of her breast into his skillful mouth. Qasim's reaction was immediate as a low sound vibrated up from his gut. Vectra felt him squeeze her hips an instant before she was tossed to her stomach upon the bed. Her nails clutched at the shiny black-and-white fabric of the comforter. Her back arched sharply when his teeth scraped her hips and the curve of her derriere.

"Sim . . ." she moaned into the cushiony bed covering, lifting her bottom reflexively when his palms slipped beneath her thighs to draw her back. Vectra felt him settle in behind her, lying flat on his stomach, as well.

She melted, feeling his nose at the curve of one butt cheek. Then his tongue was teasing the hollow area between. His hold tightened when she jerked, sensually startled by the location of his tongue. He probed her intimately, teasing and then extending his reach to drive into her channel.

Vectra sobbed her pleasure into one of the pillows that cradled her face. He'd loosened his hold on her hips, allowing her to buck and sway more freely. She cried his name when he brought his fingers back into the act. Skimming her folds, he ruthlessly delved inside while stirring her clit beneath the wide pad of his thumb.

Qasim worked her deftly, all the while easing up to shelter Vectra beneath him and savagely kicking off the rest of his clothes along the way. A soft rustling of plastic merged in with labored breathing and hoarse cries. Qasim cringed while easing protection over a painfully rigid erection. Still, he was able to take her with care. Once tightly enveloped in her sheath, he lost any ability for restraint.

Vectra reached up to hook her hand around Sim's neck, her fingers grazing the silken hair at his nape. Hips rocked and bucked on a slow, strong rhythm that forced throaty moans past their mouths. Flat beneath Qasim on the bed, Vectra plummeted and tumbled into an abyss of sensation she had no wish to find her way out of.

■ ■ ■ ■

"So how long does it take for one person to pick all these?"

Vectra smiled, her hand pausing over the vine she crouched before. She collected a few more of the plump grapes. "I don't know since I've never done it. There's always a first time, though." She straightened, looking out over the unending rows of healthy crop.

"This section of Carro is a private orchard for family use." She pointed toward the southwest portion in the distance. "There's other produce grown here. Besides us, the employees and their families are welcome to collect here at no charge."

"Why'd you leave?" Qasim asked, taking no further interest in the crops.

She turned, frowning. "Didn't you get my note on the pillow?"

"Something about business at the vineyard."

Smiling, Vectra turned back to the vine. "End-of-the-month business — more than usual since I've been preoccupied lately."

"And it couldn't wait?" he asked.

"I was serious last night when I said we needed to talk." She bowed her head. "I didn't think we'd be able to do that in your hotel room."

Qasim moved toward one of the vines and plucked off a plump red grape. "This okay to eat?" A sly grin tugged at his mouth.

Vectra picked up her bucket. "There's a rinsing spicket at the end of this row."

"Why'd you leave this morning?" he asked again while they walked between the tall vines clustered with the sweet fruit.

"I told you I —"

"No, after you told me about Will. Why'd you leave?"

"I was afraid."

"Of me," Qasim said the words as though her confession was no surprise.

"No, Qasim, no I —" She clutched the front of the plaid shirt she wore. "I was afraid of myself, of what kind of weird issues had followed me without me even being aware of it."

Qasim slowed his steps. "What weird issues, V?"

She hesitated and then hurled the bucket of grapes to the ground.

"V?" Sim started for her, halting when she waved him off.

Moments passed with only the wind and birdsong accompanying the rustle of leaves against the stems.

"These are . . . issues my family doesn't even know about."

"About Keith Freedman?" he stiffened when the name passed his lips.

"Remember when I told you he was more interested in my money than in who was interested in me?" She smiled tightly when he nodded.

"I found out how true that was when I went with him to Miami and he got a taste of the power money could provide. His family worked for mine right here on this vineyard. They never had much, and he . . . he wanted to change that, and I wanted to help. I had the gallery going here, and I gave him the money to get something going on his own. That didn't work out so well. Keith went through everything I gave him and expected more. I'd been running this place. I had the gallery in the city, and the Miami place was shaping up to be another success."

She spent a few moments staring up at the sky. "It was safe to say I knew what I was talking about businesswise — at least a little. Keith didn't think so, and he didn't mind letting me know how much."

Qasim massaged his collarbone while working a muscle along his jaw. He strode to the spicket and doused his face with the cool water. "I don't know how Oliver and Mr. B could let that fool get away with that."

"They knew enough." Vectra sighed. "They threatened to kill him for it, but left him alone because I asked them to."

He blinked, thick lashes spikey with moisture as he watched her. "Why would you do that?"

"Because I didn't want the two men I love most in the world behind bars. I learned how to keep my mouth shut about the way he handled money. I *tried* to learn, anyway."

Qasim felt the rage beginning to catch fire like kindling. Thoughts of Vectra in that situation ran wild in his head. "We need to change the subject, V." He spread the lingering water from his face through his hair. "What does this have to do with why you left? Because you had to step in and tell me about what was going on with Will? Did you think I'd react to something like that the way that idiot did?"

"No, Sim. You don't remind me of Keith at all. Your situation with Will reminded me of who *I* was with Keith — when someone I cared about was in a bad place and I wanted to help. Your situation took me back to a place I wasn't expecting, a place I thought I was done with. *That* was what scared me."

She hugged herself as though she were

shivering in the midst of the late morning sun. "I was afraid of messing up, having us not make it because I'd overstepped."

Qasim moved before her, blocking her path when she would've paced off. "Do you think any of the crap that fool took you through was your fault?"

"I know it wasn't, but getting my head and my heart on the same wavelengths was harder than I thought, and I thought I'd licked it until I had to admit what I wanted from you."

He tweaked her chin, lifting it a bit. "What are you trying to tell me, V?"

"That I was afraid — afraid I'd screw up over nothing . . . And then sharing with you all that creep put me through before I — I needed you to know, but couldn't make myself say the words. After all that I went through with Keith, I swore I'd never be controlled by fear ever again and not being able to talk to you about this . . . that fear came down out of nowhere."

Qasim grazed his knuckles along her cheek. "Honey, don't you think I'm afraid, too?"

"Maybe, but you're not coming from where I am."

"Really? After what I told you about how often people have let me down? Maybe I came to expect it so much that I couldn't see anything else. My *issues* with possessiveness didn't fit when it came to you. That became even clearer when Oliver told me what that fool did to you. I knew I had no place having anything to do with you.

"I knew it and I said 'to hell with it.' *And* since being your friend doesn't appeal to me even a little bit . . ." he smiled, pulled her into him when she returned the gesture ". . . you being my *ex*-lover is just wrong in too many ways to name."

Vectra's smile remained, though her eyes tinged with just a hint of curiosity. "Will you promise to tell me when I'm getting weird on you?"

Qasim locked his arms about her waist. "Only if you promise to do the same for me."

"Promise." Vectra stood on her toes, sharing with him a kiss of desire and love.

"So what now?" Vectra nuzzled her cheek against Qasim's grizzled jaw.

"Well, I'm invited to a pretty good party tonight," he suggested.

Vectra laughed. "This all got started because of a party."

"And to think, I almost didn't go." Qasim grinned.

"Me, too." Vectra beamed. "Guess we

needed a good reason."

"Yeah . . . but I've always been a fan of a good party." Qasim outlined her ear with the tip of his nose and then set his mouth against it. "Especially the kind that come after weddings."

She blinked, swallowed. "Yeah, those are, um . . . pretty good. I haven't been to a party like that in a long time."

"Neither have I."

"Let me know if you hear of one?"

"Count on it, Ms. Bauer." He leaned in as if to kiss her and then seemed to reconsider. "So what else goes on in a vineyard besides picking grapes?"

"Why, Mr. Wilder, what are you insinuating? I'm a good girl." She huffed. "Picking grapes is all I've ever done out here."

"That's a pity." Qasim hoisted her against his chest. "Let's see what we can do to change that."

Vectra's laughter carried until Qasim found a perfect, private spot amidst the healthy vines. He silenced her more sweetly than she could ever have imagined.

ABOUT THE AUTHOR

AlTonya Washington has been a romance novelist for nine years. Her novel *Finding Love Again* won the RT Reviewers' Choice Award for Best Multicultural Novel in 2004. Her 2012 title *His Texas Touch,* second in the Lone Star Seduction series, won the RT Reviewers' Choice Award for Best Harlequin Kimani Romance. She enjoys being a mom and librarian in North Carolina.